The Lingering Solitude
of the Girl on the Moon
(and Other Single-Serving Stories)

Chester Tanyeo

The Lingering Solitude of the Girl on the Moon
(and Other Single-Serving Stories)

ISBN **978-981-11-0761-0**

First Edition: 15th September 2016 (Mid-Autumn)

The Lingering Solitude of the Girl on the Moon
(and Other Single-Serving Stories)

Published by noctalis.com

Singapore

nocturne.noctalis.com

This is a work of fiction. Names, characters, locations and events are either the product of the author's imagination, or, if real, used fictitiously.

A Box of Lucky Things: A Love Story

"The government believes, by imposing a hundred dollar entry fee on the casino, gamblers wouldn't go. They can't possibly win, because they start off with a loss." She holds the end of the long spoon between thumb and fingertip, dangling it almost, pressing, slowly, into the ice-cream.

He leans forwards, over his coffee. "You know, possibly because we did it here, other countries are thinking about doing it too. Have an entry fee. It serves a political purpose."

"Political?"

"No government wants to be seen as introducing a vice. They want the money a casino would bring, but they can't be seen as encouraging gambling, as being a root cause of the inevitable sob stories of families torn apart by debt. This way, they look as if they are discouraging the addicts; you start off with, as you said, a loss, so you can't possibly win."

"It shows a fundamental lack of understanding of gambling addiction. Gamblers don't play because they win – they like it, of course – but really, while gamblers may play to win, gamblers *keep playing* because they want to stop losing. An entry fee gives them a loss they have to make up before they've gotten started. I imagine many of those who walk through the door do so thinking of the hundred dollars they *absolutely* have to make back."

"Do you gamble?"

"No. I believe in something gamblers cannot believe in. Gamblers believe in luck."

"And you don't?"

"Not the way gamblers do." She looks away, thinks. "It's like... Random things happen. People don't really understand how many things are happening, all around, all the time. Like if I speak a little louder, someone near by might hear a word and remember something important. And they'd think it's luck. But it's a natural consequence of the sheer number of things happening. Since a billion things are happening, some of those things would have to be favourable to some people, some of those things will be lucky. I don't believe in luck, I believe in probability. Which means you don't bet on one out of ten thousand numbers coming up when the prize doesn't even pay close to ten thousand dollars."

"I see."

"There's no such thing as luck, there's only statistics."

He smiles. "That's very true."

"Do *you* gamble?"

"No. Oh. Since it's a first date, I should be entirely explicitly honest. Chinese New Year or when friends play. Socially. Does this bother you?"

"No."

"Okay."

She smiles. "If it did, would you stop?"

"Sure."

"Really? Just like that?"

"Yeah. It's not that important to me. I mean, if we continue dating, obviously."

"Obviously."

"Hmm."

She smiles.

"Yeah."

She shrugs. "Um. There's this story about a lucky charm, like, it brings supernatural luck, but it can only be sold for less than you paid for it."

"Oh?"

"I can't quite remember it. Now it's going to bother me all night."

He laughs. "Well, I can think of something else to bother you all night."

"Oh sweetie. Did you expect that to work?"

"No, but not saying anything certainly wouldn't."

She laughs. "Okay."

"I'm told it doesn't matter how lame the line is if the girl is interested, so I assume it doesn't matter how good the line is if the girl isn't."

"Maybe the girl isn't sure she's interested, it being the first time we're meeting, and so a lame line kinda makes her think she's not."

"Good point. You know, I understand it happens, but I always thought things shouldn't hinge on just one line. As if the course of lives are so easily turned... one line, spoken at the right moment, or not spoken. I understand it happens, but I don't like that it does."

"When things hinge on just one line... that's like luck."

"Yes."

She reads his text: The story you were talking about. It's called the bottle imp. It's a monkey's paw not a rabbit's foot.

I don't know what's a monkey's paw

We'll talk about it later. Dinner. 7 ok?

You're persistent. 8 if you pick me up from work

"A rabbit's foot is an object which is lucky. A monkey's paw is something which grants wishes, but in a bad way, like, if you wish for money, you get the life insurance after someone dies."

"You said the bottle imp is a monkey's paw?"

"It is, it grants wishes. But the story isn't about the wishes. It's about the bottle itself. There are conditions. If the owner dies, his soul will burn in Hell for eternity. The bottle may not be given or thrown, only sold, or it'd find its way back. It can only be sold for coin, never paper currency, and, most importantly, it can only be sold for less than the owner paid for it."

"You read the story?"

"I found the wiki, though I think I should still get points for trying. Robert Louis Stevenson. There's this interesting paradox. No one will buy it for one cent, since you won't be able to sell it. No one will buy it for two cents, knowing they can't sell it for one cent."

She nods.

"So, the paradox goes, no one will buy it for three cents, because no one would buy it for two cents, so if you buy it for three you wouldn't be able to sell it. And the paradox keeps going, so no one will buy it at any price."

"But…"

"I know, right? The logic is sound, but clearly people would buy it."

She shrugs. "The fundamental flaw in the paradox is the assumption people do the logical thing. People generally don't."

"That's true."

"Would you?"

"Sure."

"At three cents?"

"Maybe. I don't like these hypothetical questions, these would you give a blowjob for a million dollars questions. I don't think we really know until we're in the moment."

"I would, I think, even at two cents, maybe. Just to find out if such a thing is real."

"But you don't believe in luck, so it can't be real."

"Yes, but I want to believe in magic."

"Okay, here's the plan."

She raises an eyebrow. "There's a plan?"

"We are going to find a lucky charm. A rabbit's foot, a bottle imp."

"Say what now?"

"It's something we can do together. Not right now. Maybe tomorrow."

She laughs. "When you first said you had a plan... I was afraid you had some weird after sex thing."

"No, I'm good. You were... adequate."

"Idiot. So what are we doing tomorrow?"

"Well, for such a thing to exist, it must be old, because it can't be lucky if it can't take care of itself."

"So you want to go find an old... rabbit's foot?"

"It doesn't have to be a rabbit's foot. It could be a horseshoe. Or whatever it is we're supposed to find lucky. What do Chinese people find lucky? Red? Gold? I never thought about it before."

"Red and gold. Dragons, phoenixes."

"Pandas."

"I don't think so, black and white, unlucky."

"Cute though."

"So fat, so furry, you kinda want to hug them."

"Which would be unlucky for you. How lucky can they be, since they're going extinct?"

"But they're not yet extinct, so that's lucky."

"True."

"Hmm."

"…"

"…"

"What were we talking about? Oh right, my plan. We find a lucky charm. You know, red and gold, we seem to find traits lucky, instead of actual things. Anyway, I don't think a lucky charm has to be in the form of a traditional lucky charm. The only thing I'm certain of is it has to be old. Can you think of any other criterion?"

"I don't know. If someone says it's lucky?"

"That's a quick way to get conned. Lucky charms are like 'detox', an easy label to separate the gullible from their money. It's the same reason why those scam emails are always written in bad English."

"There's a reason they're in bad English?"

"Yes. So what do you think about the plan?"

"Find a lucky charm?"

"Yeah. It's something we can do together."

"That's the dumbest thing I've ever heard. I'm totally in."

She says: "I thought about what you said, about lucky charms. What else it has to be besides old."

"Okay."

"The easiest example of luck is in a casino, right? Say, um— roulette. There are sixty numbers or whatever. Bunch of people place their numbers. But the ball can only land on one number. I know more than one person can place on one number, but people generally don't. So if ten people play, we know who's the luckiest, but we don't know who the second luckiest is. All the losers are equally losers. And maybe the winner isn't the luckiest, because it's a zero sum game, in a sense, the ball can only land on one number, maybe he's not the luckiest, and he's the *least unlucky*? Does this make sense?"

"I think so. You're talking about luck as a quantifiable thing, as a number, and unluck, I suppose, as some sort of opposing force?"

"Say I'm driving and I avoid a cat, the cat is lucky, but if, in avoiding the cat, I knock into someone, whoever I knock into is unlucky, right? Or are they just a helpless bystander, a victim of the cat's luck?"

He thinks a moment. "I think I understand what you're saying."

She nods.

"Our first date, you said something. You said random events happen and just by the nature of things, some random events would be favourable to some people."

"You remember."

"I like it. I like that you can be, that you are, skeptical and thinking and yet talk about luck as if it really existed."

"Just because something doesn't exist doesn't mean we can't talk about it. You know that."

"People don't always do the logical thing. You also said that on our first date."

"Our second. It was just last week."

"But if we're going to find a charm, doesn't it mean we believe luck is real? Because, if it isn't, a charm can't exist, and you shouldn't go looking for something which can never be found."

"We're going to find a charm because it's fun. We're not supposed to actually find it."

"Ahh! That makes more sense."

She smiles. "It bothers you, doesn't it? When your actions don't make sense. It's like you have to be able to explain yourself to yourself."

"Everyone has to explain themselves to themselves."

"Less than you'd think. A lot less than you'd think."

She says: "I realise something. It doesn't only have to be old, it has to be small, right?"

"Yes. Something old, something small. Something you can put in a pocket."

"Or something you can wear." She runs her fingers over old silver rings. "How do we tell if they're lucky? Because all I can tell is some of them are rather pretty."

She stops before the open door of the Ferris wheel cabin. "You first."

"Are you afraid of heights? We don't have to ride it."

"It's fine. But you sit next to the door."

"You know if something happens and you're hanging on, I can pull you in, but you can't pull me in."

"IS something going to happen?"

He laughs. "Of course not."

"Then you first."

They settle. The machine rumbles to slow ascent. She looks around nervously, he looks at her.

He smiles. "I'm just saying the person most qualified to do the pulling should sit where the pulling can be done. It's meritocratic."

"You ever notice how the people most enthusiastic about meritocracy are rich people?"

"I only hear the term mentioned by the government."

"Yes, rich people."

"Fair point."

"As a system, meritocracy is great. Obviously, as a principle, the alternative is you know, nepotism or racism or whatever, things which are not great. You know how we don't have a word for 'not murdering'?"

"Err?"

"We don't have a word to say someone isn't killing someone or has never killed someone. You don't introduce someone and say 'This is John, he's not a rapist.'"

He laughs. "Okay."

"The alternatives to meritocracy are all bad things, so why do we have a word for 'meritocracy'? It shouldn't have a word, it's common sense. It's simply the best way for things to be done. The job goes to the person best able to do it, regardless of race, language or religion."

"People like naming things. There's a word which means 'throwing someone out of a window'. Though I admit there isn't a word for not being thrown out of a window. As far as I know."

"What word means…?"

"Defenestration."

"Defenestration?"

"Yeah."

"Then clearly the word for not being thrown would be 'fenestration'."

"Logical, but 'fenestration' means 'opening'. Defenestration means to de someone through an opening, specifically a window. But I get your point."

"What's my point?"

"Meritocracy is common sense."

"Oh right. Okay. There's this experiment see, two people play Monopoly. One person is randomly chosen to start with more money. As the game progresses, they extend their lead. It becomes clear they're winning, crushing their opponent. They start to talk louder, sit with their arms and legs open, move things on the table so they have more space. The scientists placed a bowl of snacks on the table, in between both players. At least one winner picked up the bowl, effectively, well… monopolising the snack."

"So winners become assholes."

"That's the point of the experiment, to show winners are assholes, why BMW drivers are the worst. It's called an empathy gap. How those at the top cannot empathise with those at the bottom."

He looks at the queue for the ride, far below them. "When you're waiting, all you know is you're waiting. When you're sitting here, you forget what it means to wait."

"I'm waiting to get off this deathtrap."

"Keep talking, it'll take your mind off how high in the air we are, with only a thin sheet of metal between your feet and a great looming drop."

Her sudden annoyance melts into a smile. "You are such an asshole."

"Empathy gap, apparently."

"I was talking about the experiment because at the end of the interview, all of the winners attribute their winning to skill. If they care to mention the head start at all, it's only to dismiss it. Like, you know, 'The head start mattered, but not really.' In their head, it's all because of skill. They earned their victory."

"I see."

"Which is the problem with meritocracy. The system is fine, but the word so often gets used as a narrative, rich people saying they are rich because they've earned it. Saying the system works because it allows people like themselves to earn wealth. But when they say that, they're also saying, 'if you're poor, it's your fault'. And meritocracy is the political cover to allow them to blame the poor for being poor. The experiment kinda shows they believe it, that it's human nature for anyone who is rich to think they've earned it, but the fact is, nobody is rich on hard work alone. Millions of people work hard. The poorest often work the hardest. It takes more than hard work."

"Opportunity." He smiles, does the thing he does with his eyebrow when he thinks he's being clever. "Luck."

"Yes! And skill and talent and fortitude. Some combination of all these things, and few of those things are earned. Meritocracy allows the poor man's son to become rich, it's true. But now he's rich, he's uses the word to explain why his brother is still poor. Whatever luck he had – starting the right business, getting the degree just when an industry is booming – any luck is dismissed, matters but doesn't really matter, like the head start in the Monopoly experiment. Rich people talk about meritocracy because it means they deserve their wealth."

He nods.

"And then they say things like handouts are 'unmeritocratic'. That people have no incentive to work if we have welfare. Then 'meritocracy' becomes another reason – yet another *justification* – for the rich to keep the poor poor."

"I've always wondered how meritocracy works for the single mom who can't get a house, for the person who works two jobs because his wife has a chronic disease. There may be equal opportunity for jobs, but not everyone is equally positioned to take them."

They are silent, for a while.

Then he says, his voice musing: "If meritocracy works so well, why do we have an income disparity – the distance between the very rich and the very poor – amongst the highest in the world?"

He says, as he drives: "I suddenly realised I thought of this before. A few years ago I thought of making luck batteries."

"Luck batteries?"

"Ang baos are lucky, right? So if you collect them, press them together, it attracts more luck. Because of gravity."

"Gravity?"

"Gravity requires mass. You need a critical mass of ang baos. Once you have it, it attracts more luck."

"So did it work?"

"I never actually made one. Was afraid I'd forget and throw it away without taking out the money. So I took out the money."

"It's the ang bao which is lucky, not the money."

"No no no. Ang baos are lucky because it's free money. Once you take out the money, it's not lucky anymore."

"Ah. Are we going to collect ang baos?"

"Might as well. We don't qualify once we're married."

"Once we're married?"

"I'm not proposing. But if we're still together in a few years, yeah... It's not like I'm planning the wedding, so don't freak out, I mean, it's what couples do, right? It's the natural course of events."

"..."

"Are you freaking out? I can't see your face when I'm driving."

"I'm not. I'm thinking. How many years are we talking about?"

She says: "No. You can't 'have a good feeling' about this. There has to be something about it which other people can understand. Your feelings aren't important, this isn't tumblr."

"But you've been buying whatever you like."

"It's not my fault you take me shopping."

"Okay, new rule. One item per trip, something we both agree on."

"Okay."

"How about that? It's old, it's not very small, but we can start over."

She gives the old wood a pat. "This will be our lucky box, then."

He says: "So you have the huat, the luck. Then you have the suay, the unluck. And it combines together into a sort of ying-yang thing, like Pisces."

"Wouldn't it mean your luck is neutral and nothing happens?"

"If it were in equilibrium, yes. But one should cultivate the huat and repress the suay. After you told me about your 'maybe he's not lucky, maybe the other guy is unlucky' thing, I understand Chinese luck more. You see, it's not *just* four-leaved clovers and horseshoes for us. We have things which are lucky, red, and things which are unlucky, black. Luck and unluck are two distinct, contrasting forces, locked in eternal conflict. It's the duality. So you have the huat and you have the suay."

"We're not the only ones with unlucky. There's like black cats and broken mirrors."

"Oh right. Even better. Than the huat and the suay applies to everyone at all times."

"I suppose it does." She smiles. "If luck existed at all."

She fishes the tiny glass monkey out of her bag, places it on the table. "You put condoms in our box. You can't do that."

"Take them out then."

She tosses one at him.

He grins. "They do call it 'getting lucky'."

She tosses another.

"Ohh, well..."

She tosses one more.

"Now you're just overestimating me."

"I dare to dream. What are we going to do once we find a lucky charm?"

"We're never going to find one. If we did, we'd have to stop looking, and then what would we do?"

"Isn't it obvious? We find another one."

She says: "This one."

"I know it's supposed to be a dragon, but it kind of looks like a cow."

"It doesn't. Dragons are lucky."

"It does. Look at it. It's dragon-coloured, but it's a cow. It's a dracow."

"It's not a dracow. There's no such thing."

"Of course there is. You're holding one."

She says: "We have gone to every flea market and second hand shop in the country."

"Yes."

"Three years now."

"Uh-huh."

"All we have is a box of trinkets."

"It's clearly working."

"Huh?"

"I have you."

"Aw. But you had me before we started this."

"Literally. I had you literally. I literally had you."

"Okayy... You had sex. Congrats."

"Thank you."

"The girl you had sex with happens to be your girlfriend. Shocker of a plot twist."

"Still counts."

"Stop grinning like that. I don't know if I should be flattered or insulted."

"Why?"

"I don't know. It just feels that way and anyway it makes no sense. It's not a conquest if the gates are open and you can just walk in."

He shakes his head. "No. It's not a conquest at all. I'm not going to stop trying to impress you. I'm not going to stop winning you just because you're already won. It doesn't matter how easy it is, I will win your heart over and over. And I think I'm entitled to celebrate every time I do."

"Oh. Um. Okay then. But what about the box of stuff? Any one of them could be a lucky charm. Shouldn't we start testing them instead of buying more?"

"I haven't figured out how to test."

"We go to a casino?"

"I'm not paying two hundred bucks."

"It's only a hundred."

"I'm not going without you."

"Okay. Go buy lottery."

"No, the sample size is too small. You have to try a few times."

"You don't. You wear a piece and you try your luck and if you don't win it's not lucky so it gets taken out."

"You have to try a few times."

"You don't."

"You're talking about elimination, we need a group thing, where everyone gets pitted against everyone else."

"That would take forever."

"Which is why lottery is out. How about we do the thing where we throw them away and if they come back they're lucky?"

"They're not going to come back. Someone is going to find them and be lucky for finding them."

"How about this then?" He picks up the box, places it on the bed, pulls out the scarf which serves as a covering, moves behind her. "I'm going to blindfold you."

"Um…"

He fiddles. He fumbles.

"Er… Are we having sex?"

"No no, but your eyes have to be closed."

"The cloth is too short to tie, isn't it?"

"Yeah. Lean your head back so it doesn't fall off."

"Really? Can't I just close my eyes?"

The bed shift as he moves. "If these are all lucky, then whatever you choose has to be the luckiest." He guides her hand into the box. "Choose carefully. There's three years of you and me in here."

Her fingers run over figures, a rabbit, a tortoise, the smoothness of porcelain and the cool of brass, her fingers run over stones of, she remembers, jade, opal, onyx. "Three years of you and me." Her fingers run over silver rings, many many silver rings, plain rings and rings with stones and one of intricate metal ivy. "This one." She holds up a ring.

She feels him take the ring, feels his hand cover hers, feels the metal slide onto her finger.

"Three years of you and me."

The cloth over her eyes falls as her head moves forwards. She looks at the ring around her finger, silver and shiny, then up into his bright bright eyes.

And he says: "I... um– I'm not sure how to do this."

She shakes her head. "You don't have to."

"But I need to... you know, ask the question."

She nods, rapidly, fervently. "You already have."

He grins, and with that grin the world seems a very small place, small as a ring around a finger, just large enough for two people.

She softens, if she could soften any further, at how relieved he had been. "You have to choose a ring too."

He lifts his hand. "I already did."

She reaches for her ring, turns it on her finger. "It fits perfectly."

"Lucky, isn't it? This would be so much more awkward if it didn't."

"Lucky," she smiles.

And his eyes shine. "But you don't believe in luck."

"I don't have to. I think now I believe in magic."

As he sleeps, she carefully leaves their bed, picks up the box, goes to the bathroom.

She smiles as she looks at the ring on her hand, as she pulls it free, as she places it on the counter.

She opens the box, picks a ring at random, slips it on.

It fits.

It fits perfectly.

(In time to come, she'd occasionally open the box, the figures and stones now lining the side, so the rings would have all of the centre; she'd open the box and she'd slide off her ring and she'd put another one on. Maybe he notices, maybe he doesn't, but neither of them says anything.)

But the thing she can't figure out is how he got her to choose a ring, out of a box full of random stuff.

There were a lot of rings in there – she liked rings – but he would have been certain, wouldn't he?

Someone who knew the only way to get whichever ring she choose to fit – the only way to get *one ring* to fit – is to get *all the rings* to fit. He had had them all resized. Someone who knew that, someone who went to all that trouble so a perfect moment wouldn't be interrupted by a ring of the wrong size, he would have been certain she'd choose a ring.

She takes off this ring, puts the proper one back on.

He would have been certain, wouldn't he?

Or maybe it's just luck.

She doesn't know.

But still she smiles.

She smiles so hard she cries.

The Lingering Solitude of the Girl on the Moon

On the night of Mid-Autumn, he sits alone at home.

He sits alone at home and he sends her his very first message.

Hey. I love that too! We should be friends.

On the night of Mid-Autumn, when the moon is best and brightest, she leans against the railing.

She leans against the railing and she says: "Why are you standing so close?"

"I was here first, you stood next to me."

"Oh."

He looks up. "The moon goddess isn't really a goddess you know."

"She's just a girl who lives there." She looks at the moon too. "Do you think she gets lonely?"

"She has her rabbit."

"Yeah."

They're quiet, the good kind of quiet.

She says: "Can you describe loneliness?"

He nods at the distant moon. "There's this moment.

"There's this moment. The girl laughs and she giggles and she squirms a tiny bit which I see in her shoulders, her head looks down and her eyes look up, her eyes look up and they look into mine and they are luminous and I realise I'm smiling. I realise I've said something which may be clever but it's not clever enough to be funny but she's laughing anyway. She's giggling and it's not because it's clever but because she's happy. I somehow have this magical ability to make her happy and it's such a great thing because I want her to be happy so much.

"She's my favourite person in all the vastness of this blue earth and I want to be her favourite person too. I want her to like me and I know she does but I want her to like me even more. I must be awesome because why else would a girl this magical be here with me, right now. I must be awesome and I feel great.

"There's this moment and it is delight and wonder and joy and more of all those things because life is dreary and dull, full of schedule and routine, devoid of delight and wonder and joy. Now, right now, life doesn't feel that way, doesn't feel like the passing of time. The subtle realisation flows through me; intimacy is not having someone to talk to as your unguarded self, intimacy is not sex, intimacy is not a future shared, intimacy is all these things, but most of all intimacy is this moment in between these things, it is this moment of wonder, this moment of warmth and comfort and safety, of knowing I'm in the right place, of knowing everything I say will be funny and everything I do will be sweet, my every touch will be accepted, my every act returned, my every feeling shared.

"This moment in between the past we've had and the future we'll have, this moment shining. This moment which isn't alone, isn't isolated, isn't special at all, it is only one shining moment in a life already full with shining moments and with so many more to come."

He turns to her, she's almost laughing. "That's not loneliness at all!"

"Loneliness is the understanding you will never feel that again."

"Oh!" She frowns-pouts. "That's so sad."

"Except it isn't, loneliness doesn't destroy you. It fucks you over, kills a piece of your soul, but it doesn't fuck you over enough you cannot ignore it, pretend it's not there and go on with your life, like a person walking and bleeding and walking anyway, as if you aren't dripping a trail of droplets of inner self. The loneliness is just another piece of emptiness inside an emptiness already the shape of the soul.

"We are all empty inside. We need other people to fill us, we need one special person to fill us all the way. That's what loneliness is, it is what exists when there is no one else to make the darkness beautiful, because even darkness can be beautiful, as long as someone else sees it too."

"Even darkness can be beautiful, I love that."

"I love you."

She smiles, leans forwards, kisses him quickly on the lips. She turns to the sky. "As long as someone else sees it too." She points.

"A sky lantern!" The lantern ascends, moving light against the stillness of the moon. "I've never seen one before."

"You didn't light the ones I gave you?"

"No, they're still in the car, let's go get one. That's amazing, that we see one today, I've never seen one before!"

She lies, soft and smooth and lovely, in the curve of his arm. "Remember that thing you told me not to do?"

"You did it."

"Yeah… Your dolldoll is amazing."

"And now you want to tell me how it turned out badly and you don't want me to say I told you so."

She turns.

"Ow!"

"My profile says I bite."

"You say that every time you bite me. Nobody thinks it means literally, it's misrepresentation."

"It's not."

"It is. People thinks it means something sexual, as if you like to use your mouth."

"I can tie a cherry stem in my mouth."

"That's another thing you keep misrepresenting, nobody thinks it means literally either. It's a way of saying you give good blowjobs." He gently pushes her head down.

"It isn't." She allows herself to be guided half the distance before she laughs. "I can see where this is going." She twists, sits up. "Can I tell you my story first?"

He holds her gaze as she holds his heart, with gentle certainty. He holds her gaze and he smiles. "Happy anniversary, doll."

She grins. "Happy anniversary."

"So tell me about the stupid thing you did."

On the night of Mid-Autumn, when the moon is best and brightest, they sit on the bench by the shore of the lake.

They sit on the bench by the shore of the lake and they are quiet.

He looks across the waves of the water. "The lake is ever changing but the moon never changes."

Her voice is soft and it is lovely. "The moon is always changing and the lake is always changing, but the lake will always reflect the moon."

"Except she doesn't. She can't. She hides her face with her hair, her face changes as her hair moves, but it doesn't mean her face is changing. She only promises to change, she doesn't really, she can't, some people can't."

She is silent. He doesn't turn to look at her, his eyes never leave the lake.

When the quiet gets too quiet, he says: "The moon goddess."

"Yes?"

"Is she alone because she wants to live on the moon, or does she live on the moon because she wants to be alone?"

"I don't know."

"Does she want to be alone?"

"No."

"But she wants to live on the moon."

"Yes."

"And neither will change."

"Neither can."

He does not say: "The distance between the lake and the moon is so so great, yet they are forever joined by the beam of a star. You sit next to me but we no longer have our bridge across the sky." He says: "Let's go, it's getting late."

"Okay." They stand, he picks up the plastic debris the mooncake came in, they walk.

"Do you want to come over?"

"I've to work tomorrow."

"Of course you do."

On the drive back–

"One day I'll stop asking. We barely even meet anymore. One day that will stop too. Then we'll stop talking."

"Let's not do this again."

"You always win, when we argue. You give me reasons and then I spend months addressing them and it turns out those reasons weren't real, you only said them to win. You say logical things but they're not true."

"Let's not do this again."

"You're right. As usual. One day you'll be right and you'll be alone."

At her door–

"Will you get lonely?"

"Yes."

"But you won't change."

She shakes her head, leans forwards, kisses him quickly on the lips. "Some people can't."

"Yeah."

She holds his gaze as she holds his heart, barely, with timid uncertainty. "Will you be lonely?"

"I already am, doll."

Her smile no longer lights up her eyes. "Sorry."

"Yeah, well." He fails to smile too. "I'm tired."

She nods. "Me too."

The door closes and she is gone.

He drives home alone.

He drives home alone and he remembers that very first message.

We should be friends.

And we were, weren't we? We were.

We were—

The very best of friends.

On the night of Mid-Autumn, the moon hangs in the sky, when she is best and brightest.

Changer unchanging, alone.

(She has her rabbit.)

Witch-Girl: A Bagful of Starlight

"All things can have meaning," she says; "it is the nature of things."

Ramiel: "Valentine's Day is next week."

Stacey: "Is it?"

"What do you want to do?"

"For Valentine's? Nothing. It's a made-up holiday to sell overpriced cliches. And the concept of obligatory sex is offensive to women and *I*, as a woman, am offended."

"Surely that doesn't apply to you. You use sex as a weapon."

"Rubbish. I never withhold sex."

"Whenever you do something wrong and I want to talk about it, you suddenly get very... excited."

"Lies and slander. I never do anything wrong." She winks. "Particularly when it comes to sex."

"Anyway, it's our first Valentine's Day as a couple. We should do something. Like normal people."

"I'm a witch. You're a demon. You should just give up on being normal. Seriously."

"It's normal for a demon. There's Valentine's Day in Hell. It's a few hundred years old."

"What's it like?"

"As you said, overpriced gifts. But still, a day to celebrate love. It's a beautiful idea."

She sighs. "Do you know who Saint Valentine is?"

"Not really."

"Accounts differ. But there's nothing about love. He was just a Roman priest who got beaten and beheaded for refusing to renounce Christ. There's nothing romantic about it. It's pretty generic, even by the standards of martyr stories. In some stories, he married Christian couples, but that's the closest it gets. It's hardly Romeo and Juliet."

"So we won't be doing anything for Valentine's?"

"We'll be doing what we'll normally be doing."

"That's not very fun."

"It's just a day. It doesn't mean anything."

She lies with her head upon his chest. He lightly pushes her hair away from the back of her neck, revealing her mark: the outline of a heart. Anastasia Valentine, with a heart on her neck, who likes love stories but doesn't want to celebrate the day which shares her name.

She turns over to face him, lies on her arm on his chest. "You're thinking about me."

"How do you know?"

She shrugs. "I know."

Silence, for a moment.

"Do you remember; when we went for the Diwali festival and they had those little candles? Small discs, really-really short candles, palm of your hand, came in bags of thirty or something?"

"They're called tealights."

"Right, those. I need two bags."

"You have normal candles." Boxes of them, black. He knows this because he had bought them. He had bought them because he had been witness to her performing a ritual with pink candles. There had been a pentacle of blood. And pink candles. Pink.*Pink.*

The ritual hadn't worked. She had assured him it had nothing to do with the colour of the candles. But he knew otherwise. If offered any selection of colours, she would choose pink. It didn't matter what the object was. Part of his job, he felt, was taking that choice away from her.

"Two bags. Got it."

At three AM on the night between February thirteenth and fourteenth, they walk through the park.

She pulls him off the lit path onto the grass. The ground slopes gently upwards and she leads him to the centre of the grass patch, surrounded by trees. It is quiet, the trees sheltering them from the wind pushing the orange clouds across the starless sky.

She releases his hand, unslings her bag, sits upon the grass, pulls out a bag of tealights. She rips the plastic open, picks up a tiny light. "Fire."

He narrows his eyes and the small candle flares to life. Leaving her bag, she walks a few steps, places the tiny light upon the grass. She picks up another tealight, repeats the process.

She pulls out the other bag of tealights and hands it to him. "Here, just place them wherever."

"Okay."

"Not wherever. Erm, equidistant from any other light."

"Okay." He ignites a tealight, hands it to her for use as a fire source and walks away.

He has placed two lights when she says: "You can't be equidistant from any other light; *every* other light. Equidistant from the nearest lights."

"Alright." He looks as she places another. She seems to be placing them randomly, a few steps apart.

He has placed another when she says: "That makes no sense."

Another two. "If it's equidistant, it'd be a grid, wouldn't it?"

Another. "What's it called when–?" ... "See? Now this is going to bother me all night."

"It's just random, Stace. Avoid clumping."

"They usually say 'clustering'. There's this colourful map thing. I'm thinking of something else... Am I?" She falls into silence.

They continue until both bags are empty. She sits, and he follows.

All around them, sixty little lights twinkle and shimmer, casting a warm glow over the grass as it slopes gently downwards. It's a beautiful sight. It makes him smile.

"It's all mangled," she says softly. She hands him a sad looking sandwich.

You have to box sandwiches, he does not say. "You made these?" he says, wondering when she did so.

"No, I bought them."

"Ah."

"I did make the tea." She pulls out a flask.

"We're having a picnic," he realises.

"This is my gift to you."

"Eh?"

"Happy Valentine's Day."

"But I didn't get you anything. You said we weren't going to–"

"No, wait. This is your gift for me. Wish me a Happy Valentine's Day."

"Huh?"

"Just say it."

"Happy Valentine's Day."

"Thank you."

The sandwich is sad and he is slightly confused. But the night is temperate and the lights are beautiful and she is shaded yellow-orange by small fires and she sits there, looking at the lights and taking small bites, thinking, always always thinking.

"This is my gift to you?" he says, just to be sure.

He sits on a hill, amidst a constellation of tealights, and the night is temperate and the sight must be beautiful but he does not look away from the girl; because the stars may be beautiful but, come moonrise, no one notices how beautiful the stars can be, because all they see is this: the stars make the moon more beautiful still.

She turns to him and she smiles and he just *loves* her. Her eyes dance in the light of the stars and her smile. "It's lovely. You did a good job."

"Thanks, one supposes. But you said Valentine's Day doesn't mean anything."

"It doesn't. But it means something to you. And you mean something to me."

So a gift to you is your gift to me. "To sit amongst the stars."

"To picnic amongst the stars. I'd have expected better sandwiches from you, but I'm not complaining."

He laughs.

She settles into a coy smile. "Can you guess what my gift to you is?"

"Isn't a gift to you your gift to me?"

"Don't be stupid. That creates infinite regression."

"I suppose it does."

"Or does it?" She taps her nose with her fingertip as she thinks. "If my gift to you is your gift to me, then I still owe you a gift, but I've already given it, so I can't owe you, except I do." Eyebrows knit. "Paradox? An infinite regression... paradox. Maybe."

"That presumes gifts are to be reciprocated."

"Gifts are."

He considers this, then nods. "Yeah, they are."

"It's a paradox," she nods. "So this is your gift to me and I still owe you a gift."

"Okay."

"Can you guess what my gift to you is?"

"Sandwiches?"

"You suck at guessing."

"So do you."

"Meh."

He sits in silence amongst the stars, looking at the moon.

They arrive back at their apartment.

He says: "Go shower."

"Later."

"I need to do something. Five minutes."

"You need to do something *now*?"

"Five minutes."

It takes him ten.

She's lying sprawled across the bed, staring up at the ceiling. "You took a while."

"You know the colourful map you were talking about?"

"Great. Now it's going to bother me again."

"It's a map showing where each point's, I suppose, area of influence is. So if you choose a random spot within that area, it'll be closer to that point than to any other point. And each line – each border – is equidistant to two points; that's the equidistance you were thinking of."

"Oh my god. Yes!"

"It's called a Voronoi tessellation."

"Ahh! Right! You looked it up?"

"I did."

"*That's* what was so important?"

"It is."

"*Why?* You don't care about such things."

"It means something to you. And you mean something to me."

She beams. She shakes her head. "That's stupid. And sweet. And lovely. You get your gift now."

"What is it?"

"It's Valentine's Day, silly, what do you think it's going to be? Obligatory sex."

They are no longer amongst the stars, but he realises you can carry the stars with you. If the right person places them there, you get to carry the stars inside your heart, like a bagful of starlight.

A bagful of starlight in the shape of a girl.

Guilty Mind

It's strange, isn't it? One day someone enters your life a stranger, one day you find yourself thinking about them, telling them things in your head, wanting to be near them. One day you realise they're your favourite person.

One day they walk out of your life and your favourite person is a stranger again.

But they're still your favourite person.

The night she walks out begins with a question.

What Israfil, Angel of the Burning Light, remembers of the moment of the Fall is this: the feather. It wafts on the air above him, rising and dipping on the breeze. He is on his back, and he reaches out for the feather as if it could somehow make sense of what had just happened. He reaches out but his hand does not cross his vision. His arms are broken, as are his legs. As are his wings. The feather is his, but, like the light shining in the sky so far above him, it belongs to him no longer.

The thing about prison is it makes people philosophical. Some people anyway.

It is lights out and I lie on the bunk above the Old Man, this philosopher with a story about a falling angel. I ask him: "And what were you before your fall?"

"I was a miner. Dirt poor, and miners know dirt. So poor my daughters tied cardboard boxes to their feet because I couldn't afford shoes. Can you imagine?"

"Never really thought of mining as something people still do. A miner, that's your life story?"

"Is it?"

He is silent, for a long time. I thought he had fallen asleep. I stare at the blue the moon makes on the wall.

Then his voice, soft though it is, cuts through the silence, giving me a small shock: "I had two daughters. The elder drowned. They say she did it to herself, but I think it was an accident."

"That's horrible. I'm so sorry."

"It was difficult, for a while, but then I forgot all about her."

"Time does that."

"Yeah it does. The time it took for her little sister to grow up enough. You ever had a young girl? About seven, eight?"

"*Had* a young girl?"

"Oh... you know exactly what I'm talking about."

The air feels dry. I swallow. "No. No, I don't."

A laugh.

"We should sleep."

"Ruby lips," he softly says. "Ruby lips."

Looking up at the ceiling, I watch the droplets fall from the shower in slow motion. Maybe I have a concussion. My head hurts, a sharp throbbing pain telling me exactly where I had hit the floor. The light on the ceiling might have looked like the sun Israfil saw. Or maybe what he saw wasn't the sun, maybe the light denied him was God, or Heaven.

A shadow crosses my vision; it is not a feather, it is the meanest face in a place of mean faces. His shoe presses into my stomach, adding another pain.

I say: "That's all."

"What do angels have to do with it?"

"I don't know. Probably nothing at all. You said to tell you what he told me. That's what he told me."

"Get up. Put some clothes on, have some self-respect."

I dress with soap still in my hair. I see Tiny in the crowd. He looks away at once. He's the only one I told about what the Old Man said. Tiny, the little rat.

They guide me to the corner the guards never go. It's an understanding between those who run the place and those who allow them to do so. I've never been sure which side are the guards, which sides are the prisoners.

The Old Man is there, on his knees. There are tears in his eyes and he is pleading. Pleading for mercy or kindness in a place emptied of both. They push me forward. He sees me. He sees the shiv which has somehow appeared in my hand.

"Finish off the sick fuck."

I shake my head. I didn't mean for this. I just told Tiny because I had to tell somebody.

The Old Man is clenching at my pants and his eyes are wild with confusion. "Why? What is this about?"

I shake my head. I want to be away. In a place where everybody wants to be away, I've never wanted to be somewhere else more.

In a place where everybody cries but nobody is supposed to, I can feel my nose clogged up, the tears blur my vision. "I'm sorry."

"I thought we were friends!"

I thought we were friends too. I thought Tiny was my friend. That's how it is. Friendship is something you think you have until the moment you realise it's not there. Friendship, mercy, kindness; these are mirages, real until you need them. I had none of these for him, I had none of these inside me.

I need to be strong but I don't feel strong. I need to be strong and so I put my foot to his shoulder and I push him to the floor. "We're not friends, you sicko."

He doesn't get up. Why bother? "Sicko? What? Why?! Because of what I said that night? That was a joke! It was a joke! Please!"

Hands shove me forward. I stumble. I like to think it was an accident but... well... it wasn't. The shiv goes into him. I am on my knees and I am killing an old man who doesn't have the strength to get to his knees. I push it further in. I pull it out.

Shivs, the way they use it here is to cut someone open, to slash not stab. It's used not like a dagger, but like a scalpel. You slash someone open, then you dig in with your fingers and you *pull*. Pull everything on the inside outside. I don't do that. Of course I don't. But I don't have to. Not for an old man.

I stand, I turn, my hands are hot wetness. I feel his hand around my ankle and I feel myself yelling. I shake my foot, I jerk it, I free myself. The faces around me are grim, but they part before me, letting me see the empty corridor behind them, giving me my out.

The last thing I see is his hand reaching out, as if I were still the friend who would save him, instead of the animal who had killed him.

It is only later, much later, when I realise: It was a joke. It really was.

"A joke?" she says. Her voice is soft, soft as the hair I idly stroke.

"Your name, Clementine. 'Oh my darling, oh my darling, oh my darling, Clementine.' Do you know the lyrics?"

"Yes."

"I didn't. After we started dating, I looked it up, wanted to sing it to you or something. Then I started to remember the things he said, the exact words. Boxes for shoes, ruby lips. It's in there, in the song, all of it. A miner has a daughter, whose name was Clementine. She wore boxes for shoes. She drowned in a river. And the miner forgot about Clementine by kissing her little sister. Everything he said, it was all in the song. The story which got him killed."

She is quiet.

I speak: "He wasn't a pedo, he was just someone who knew the lyrics to a song everyone knew but never thought about. It was a place where everyone told stories, because there was nothing else to do, stories about how we got there, what life we had lost. It must have been funny to him, to tell a children's song as if it were true. Maybe he told it before, maybe he even pretended to be a pedo before, I don't know. Maybe he thought telling me was a sign of trust. I don't know. I found out later he was three months from release. I did what I had to do. I thought I was being strong, just before I killed him I told myself I needed to be strong. It was him or me... We *were* friends. I let him down the way Tiny let me down. I sold him out to stay alive."

"Do you regret it?"

In that moment, with that question, I finally understand the story of the angel. An angel doesn't just fall, he falls because he has done something wrong. Some act for which he was thrown out of Heaven. I always thought the story was about the punishment, the fall itself, but it is a story about regret, about committing the act for which you paid with your wings, your ability to soar. The act for which you paid with your freedom, with your innocence.

I am quiet.

She speaks: "Stupid question. Of course you do."

I look at the ceiling, marked by the light from the streetlamp outside. "He had three months. I know it's not true, but sometimes I want to think he couldn't bear the thought of entering the world again, and he was too weak to kill himself, and so he told me the story so someone would do it for him."

"That's not true."

"I know."

"I have a story too."

Do you know what "mens rea" means? It's Latin, a legal term meaning "guilty mind". It's what separates a crime from an accident. Criminal intent, malice aforethought.

When I was seventeen I had my first job. "Would you like fries with that?" There was a boy there, two years older than me, the supervisor. He kept asking me out and I kept saying no. He always stood too close, I didn't like that and I didn't like him. I've never had a boyfriend before and maybe I didn't know how to deal with him, how to turn him down, how to make him stop.

When I couldn't take it anymore, I quit the job. But he started turning up, appearing at places I was at. He'd be waiting for me when I came home. Or turn up suddenly, when I went shopping. "Accidentally", you know? He would say a few words, and just be polite, and so I had to be polite too, had to say a few words too. He scared me. I remember smiling. Smiling smiling smiling, and him, him being there, just there. Polite, scary.

I told my father. He went to speak with the boy.

But he brought a screwdriver. Because he brought it, it means he intended to use it. It proves intent. Malice aforethought.

They gave him twenty years. Because he had a screwdriver.

Three months before he was to be released, he was killed in a fight.

He wasn't a miner.

But he did have a daughter.

She leaves the bed and moves across the dim light as if carried by a gentle wind.

"We've dated for close to a year," I say, because I didn't want to believe what I had just heard. But a part of me knew, a part of me didn't quite understand how and why a girl like this would be with a man like me. Why, just after my release, I had the good fortune to meet her. I've never had fortune before. A part of me had always known I still didn't.

She dresses herself in silence.

I'm not sure what to say, what to do, so I remain on the bed still radiating her warmth.

She stands at the foot of the bed, a silhouette near and out of reach. "My name isn't Clementine. It's just what my father called me. When I was a baby, he sang it to me. He said it was the only way to calm me down, to put me to sleep. All through my childhood, he sang it to me before bed. He never stopped calling me Clementine."

Her eyes hold mine. "I wasn't sure what I should do… but I had to do something. So I found the man who had killed him and I got close to him, as close to him as I could. I thought I wanted revenge, but I guess I wanted closure. I think so."

Her voice is as vacant as the bed. "I think I just wanted to hear you say you were sorry."

"I am." I look away. "You have no idea how sorry I am."

"I wanted so much for you to be a bad person... but you're not. You're kind and you work hard and you're thoughtful. And in another life I would be lucky to have you."

"In another life..."

"You're not a bad person but you're not quite a good one.

You keep saying you needed to be strong but you are weak. You were weak when you went along with your friends to the robbery and... you say you had to be strong. It was him or me, you said." She throws something onto the bed next to me, into the gulf she had vacated moments ago. A screwdriver, a line shining silver in the dim light. "It shouldn't have been him."

"I..."

"You let things happen." She looks at it, at me. "And I'm a coward too."

Weak. A coward.

This is the moment in the movie where there's a close-up, where you can see on the character's face there's been a revelation. This is the moment of epiphany, of character growth. "I am weak," I will say, and I will maybe shed a single tear or break down crying. And she'll come to me because she realises she really loves me or something.

She's right, of course, I am weak. But I didn't realise it then. I didn't react to some new understanding of the self. I reacted as, I think, anyone would: I denied it. "I'm not weak. I had no choice."

She smiles sadly. "I wanted you to be a bad person but you're not." She turns around.

Maybe she wants me to stop her. I want to. I want to call out and say I'm sorry. I want to say she's right, even if I didn't believe it. I want to say I'm weak, as if by that false confession I could draw her back.

I want to call out and say I love her.

I find myself reaching out.

I want to stop her but I am just reaching out. Silently.

And nothing happens.

Reaching out, silently, to her back as she wafts away.

Nothing happens.

Nothing happens at all.

She was lost and gone forever.

Jack and Jill

Jack and Jill went up the hill,
  to fetch a pail of water.
Jack fell down and broke his crown,
  and Jill came tumbling after.

Jill to Jack went up to check,
  to see if he was okay.
Jack was red and he was dead,
  and Jill had naught to say.

A teary Jill went down the hill,
  to the butcher shop, their home.
Placed was Jack upon his back,
  and Jill felt quite alone.

Jill looked out, and all about,
  there was no meat left to sell.
Jack she saw, upon the floor,
  and Jill thought: "Might as well."

Jill to Jack went up to hack:
  "A girl has got to eat."
Jill did cut, a broken heart,
  and Jack was sold as meat.

A Quick Explanation of Some Concepts of Politics and Democracy in a Simple Narrative

Imagine a classroom of teenagers. The teacher announces a school trip. To decide where to go, the class shouts out destinations and she writes them on the board. The class vote. Disneyland, of course, wins.

This is direct democracy. Every voter gets to vote on what is to be done.

Not everyone votes for Disneyland, so the teacher asks: "Why not?"

One guy, the guy who has no problem raising his hand and talking to the teachers, *that* guy says: "I can afford it, but I know some of us can't. I think we should go as a class. It's just not as fun if only some of us can go."

"Does anyone have a solution to this? Or would like to voice their opinion?"

The pretty girl: "We can stay at a hostel, but it will be further, we'll have less time at Disneyland." "This museum is near, we could stop by." "If some kids pay a little bit more, some can pay a little less, maybe even go for free." "I don't see why we have to stay at a hostel. They have bedbugs." "Seriously guys, the museum is really near by, we could spare a few hours."

Voices rise. Like bread. The teacher lifts a hand, snaps fingers. The class quiets. "This isn't a circus. How about you form groups with a common idea, not only on the destination, but the itinerary? It'll be easier to decide if there are less competing voices."

There's chatter. Two groups soon emerge; one with mostly rich kids, one with everyone else.

The class divide.

It happens the most vocal of the rich kids is known to be lactose-intolerant, and the poorer kids, out of spite, declare themselves to be pro-lactose. They name themselves "the pro-leta-riat". The rich kids name themselves after "So what's the opposite of milk?" "Spaghetti." "We'll call ourselves the spaghetti bourgeoisie!"

The class struggle.

A rich kid, who has joined the poor group because his best friend is there, looks over at the bourgeoisie. "Tim! Join us. Dude, what's wrong with you? If those guys win, Alan can't come."

The words "win" and "lose" quickly bubble to the surface. Like bread. Wait no.

"Joe, we should join the proletariat." "Sally, babe, it's the first time we're going to Disneyland together, I want to spend more time there." "It's not fair to the others." "Think about us." "How about a hostel, but one not so far away?" "It's the first time we can spend the night together, I don't want it to be in a hostel." "For fuck's sake, Joe. GUYS! Guys, listen, how about a hostel, but one not so far out? If we tell them the cheapest hostel is as unfair to us as staying at a hotel is unfair to them, they'll understand. That's okay right?"

In minutes, what started as two groups split into five. The names are forgotten, which is good, because nobody really agrees on how to pronounce "bourgeoisie". Some insist on "bourgeoisie", some on "bourgeois"; they don't realise those are two different words.

It quickly emerges each group has that one person. Sometimes he's the loudest. Sometimes he's the most sensible (and someone repeats what he says, but louder). Sometimes she's the quiet one who rarely speaks but always utters words of "Ohhhh"-inducing epiphany when she does. Sometimes she's the one who listens and nods and considers the concerns of every single member. They're not the same type of person, but every group has that one person. Leadership emerges.

We call members of government our "leaders". Some behave like they're our rulers, but they're wrong. Rulers are supposed to be straight and narrow. Like bread. Leaders are supposed to explain to us how what we want is unfair to other people, why we can't have nice things. They're supposed to make us agree with them, make us *want to* agree with them. Their clothes have creases because they are not supposed to iron, they are supposed to lead. They smile at jokes about heavy metal.

Many students quit their group. Some want to be leader but nobody listens to them. The museum kid leaves his group because nobody wants to go to the museum. These groupless teens go from group to group to listen to what they have to say, to listen to what the leader has to say.

Some leaders understand their own interest is never entirely the same as the group's. They argue against their own interest, they convince people who share their interest to give it up for the sake of the group. A rich kid tells another rich kid a hostel isn't really that bad.

Some leaders don't give up their own interest. Instead, they cover their self-interest with words about public interest, about the greater good. This is called "political cover". They do it so well people gather around them because they've become convinced they share that interest. The group for the most expensive hotel has some of the poorest kids.

Everyone talks about Disneyland. Only 60% voted for Disneyland in what feels like forever ago. Yet now everyone is talking about Disneyland. Everyone understands, even if they didn't want to go in the beginning, the class is going to Disneyland, so they have to get the best trip they can. Disneyland is inevitable.

This is "first-past-the-post" voting, where the single largest number wins. 60% of the vote gives you 100% of the power.

"But Sally's group wants to do that too?" "Sally also wants to stay in a hostel. Bedbugs, dude, bedbugs. Do you want bedbugs? Is that what you want?" "Well, no… but–"

To separate themselves from the other groups, positions quickly harden. The left move further to the left, the right move further to the right. The rich kids now refuse to even consider a hostel. "We're not against poor kids, we're against bedbugs. Are you saying some kids, simply because they aren't rich, ought to be fed to bedbugs? That's what you want? That's fucked up. You monster."

Promises are made. "Does Sally offer a dinosaur ride? Because we do."

The leaders start saying "we". They understand they don't speak for themselves anymore. They've become representatives, they speak for everyone in their group. They represent, yo.

"I kinda prefer Joe, you know he does charity work? He's big on philanthropy." "Big on philanthropy?" "Did I hear you guys say Joe's a philanderer?" "Joe is a what now?!"

"Museum?" "I'm sorry. We don't have the time to even listen to this." "Museum?" "No." "Museum." "If you join us, we can go for an hour, but only those who want to go." "But it's more fun if we go as a class." "The class doesn't want to go, you have to accept that. You won't get a better offer for your one vote. Maybe if you convince a few others to go before you talk to me?" The kid looks down. "I already tried that."

"I'm entitled to my opinion." "No, you're just entitled."

"If Joe would cheat on Sally, how can you trust him? How can you believe anything he says? Or haven't you heard about Joe being a philanderer?"

"Shut up, Amos."

"But the bedbugs?" "Not all hostels have bedbugs and not all hotels don't. Read a book." "I have a little sister. I need to think about the children. For the future."

This is fear-mongering. "For the children" and "For the future" are the house mottos of Phobos and Deimos. Their combined form is "For future generations". Never buy this. Anything you want for your children you already know, don't let people tell you what you *should* want. Those who sell this garbage go on so much about the things after the "for" you forget the things they're telling you to give up. You get something in the future and you don't notice *they* get something right now. They get something right now *from you*. It is often the case those who claim to want a better future for you end up being given a better present *by* you. Don't give up your present interest in return for a promised future. Promised futures almost never arrive.

"Would you like a dinosaur ride?"

This is hope-mongering. It's a term which doesn't actually exist because hope is so rarely used independently of fear. Those who monger fear always dangle hope, hope which, coincidentally and conveniently, you can buy right now. Fear only does so much, to truly bleed the desperate dry, they have to be given hope.

The bell rings for recess. The teacher, who has been marking papers while smiling quietly to herself, stands. "We'll decide after."

The teacher goes for lunch, still smiling quietly. Nobody leaves the class.

The group of kids who can't find groups look at each other and form their own group. They're not for anything, each member is just against everything else. They struggle to find a common platform. "I'm going to leave. It's better to maybe be heard in a big group with power than to be heard in a group which can't do anything." "Enough with the museum!" "I'm going to go, guys, at least if I join Joe's group I'll get a dinosaur ride." "Shut up, Amos." The group ends up with three members.

"What are you doing here, aren't you in Joe's group?" "Joe just wants to talk. Away from everyone." "Tell my ex-boyfriend to fuck off." "Does he know he's your ex? I'm not breaking up with him for you. Just go talk to him."

"Sally, babe, listen–" "You listen jerk. I've heard about your philandering ways." "What?" "That means womanising." "I know what it–" "I'm not even surprised, after what you said about feeding people to bedbugs." "I never said any of that. This is character assassination." "No, character assassination is when someone in a show is killed by a ninja. Like in that stupid cartoon you made me watch when the fat cat got stabbed by the lame duck." "The duck was walking fine." "Not lame-lame. Uncool. That uncool duck." "Okay. Listen, babe. You know the size of the groups. If both our groups join, we'll have the biggest group." "If we join, I'm guessing I have to tell my group hostels are out?" "They get a dinosaur ride." "Dinosaurs aren't real, Joe. I don't know how you're even selling that." "With fervour." "What does that even mean?" "People will believe if they believe you believe the belief you are telling them to believe. In." "Um okay?" "You just have to make like a tree." "Make like a tree and– trunk? Make like a tree and– bark!" "Dogs bark, babe. Make like a tree and believe." "Okay whatever, I stopped caring. Listen jerk, it'll be the first time we get to spend the night together, if I'm happy about it, I might be happy enough to do that thing you like."

This is corruption.

"Done! But this only works if my group joins yours, I can't go back to them and say I've entirely changed my position, you know how they feel about flip-flops." "I don't know why we hate them, they're comfortable." "Don't let anyone hear you say that. If I can't bring my group, all you'll get is one more member, which means nothing. I can sell them on a hostel if I don't call it a hostel. We find a motel, the cheapest. The guys don't want to be dicks, but they're afraid of bedbugs. I can sell a motel to my group, can you sell it to yours?" "I think so." "It'll be easier to sell if we can offer something else. What do you think about

unicorn rides? Girls like that right? You're a girl, do you think–"
"Please stop talking before I reconsider my life choices again."
"Make like a tree babe, make like a tree."

Back in the class, people are still talking.

"A circus?" "Or well, animal farm?"

"I have a little sister." "Big brother isn't always right."

"The common public fund is your money. Nobody can take it away from you." "So I can use my share to buy souvenirs?" "No, shopping isn't on the approved list." "But you said it's my money." "It is. Nobody can take it away from you." "Will I get it back?" "You get back whatever you didn't spend during the trip when it's over." "But I won't be able to shop when it's over." "It's your money, nobody can take it away from you."

"Shut up Amos." "I'm not Amos." "I know. Go find him and tell him to shut up."

News of the combined group creates a wave of scandal. The Party is now the largest group.

"Look, if the three of us find a way to combine, we'll be larger than the Party. You can't even mention 'hostel' without someone saying 'bedbugs' now anyway." "If you can forget about the water slides, I'll convince my people about a motel." "It'll take more than that." "Let's talk."

This is political compromise. This is horse-trading. Both sides get what they want, but not even close to *all* of what they want.

"Horse-trading" and "first-past-the-post" are metaphors from horse racing, a barbaric practice/sport associated with the upper class because anyone can wilfully ignore the animal cruelty which provides the goods of a modern lifestyle, but it requires wealth, and an obscene amount of it, to appreciate animal cruelty *for its own sake*. The difference between a horse and a politician is the difference between "literal" and "metaphorical": They're both full of horseshit. Also, they're both often associated with dangerously underweight professionals who are ridiculously overpaid to ride them.

"Listen guys, I don't know who died and made Tim king, but now he's saying no more water slides." "But that's why you're there!" "I know. They kicked me out because I kept protesting. They said there were too many people talking, so the three of them went off to talk alone."

This is "a disagreement on the future direction of the party". This often results in a "conflict in leadership" or a schism. This is also the "we didn't get everything we want so that guy sucks" flavour of rhetoric, also known as "haters gonna hate".

"I can convince my group of that. Are we all agreed?" "I am." "Who's going to be in charge of the combined group? Since the Party formed, Sally does all the talking. Joe just nods like a puppet." "Joe does whatever she tells him to if she will do that thing he likes." "What IS that thing he likes?" "Nobody knows. If you ask him he just smiles and sort of drifts away. Anyway–" "I heard she gets mayo and she puts it in her–" "ANYway, they're not even talking dinosaur rides anymore." "Why do people believe that? He can't pull that off! I mean, you know, he doesn't even have a dinosaur!" "Um, nobody does?" "How about we vote on who will be in charge of the combined group?" "How about we don't? For the next class trip, my guys may not want to join with your guys. Your people listen to you, my people listen to me. Let's keep it like that. We discuss amongst ourselves, and we convince our people to follow." "I can do that. This talk has been productive." "It's a brave new world."

This is a coalition, a joining of parties for a specific purpose with the understanding the combined group lasts only as long as the purpose is valid. Devastator, the awesome robot made out of smaller, less awesome robots, doesn't remain Devastator when there are no Autobots to crush into little pieces of shiny shrapnel. Like Devastator, which is made up of construction vehicles, political entities often do the opposite of what they're supposed to. Unlike Devastator, political entities tend not be awesome.

The smaller groups realise no one is going to hear them because they're too small to matter. They are quickly absorbed by the Party or the Coalition.

Except for the group against everyone, which remains against everyone, even each other. The Fringe still only has three members.

Someone does a headcount. The number ripples through the class. The Party is two votes ahead. Sally is smug. Sally is smug until Joe points at the leadership of the Coalition talking to the Fringe. "Dammit."

The three members of the Fringe have gone from no one listening to them to everyone listening to them. The Coalition make promises. The Party makes promises.

Sally realises the power of a particular kind of promise, one which the Coalition cannot offer. She pulls one of the Fringe away. "You like Mandy, don't you? You know she's my BFF." "You like *her*? Why?!" "Shut up Joe, I'm trying to work here."

The three members of the Fringe become two. It doesn't matter what the last two do, the Party has a confirmed margin of one.

Recess is over. The teacher returns to find a quieter sort of chatter. Things have settled. The lone voices have long given up. The Coalition knows it's not going to win but they're not going to join the Party anyway. They just stew and stare (They think they're moving but they go nowhere).

This doesn't mean the Party is happy. Sally isn't. Joe is. Mandy feels that special anxiety when you've agreed to something but aren't totally sure what it is you have agreed to.

The teacher: "Alright class. Have you decided anything?"

The two plans are presented. The teacher raises an eyebrow when the fighting robots are proposed. "Can I quickly see a show of hands?"

The vote is made. The Party wins.

Tim, of the Coalition, says: "Please check your phone, Miss. Raymond sent you a message." "How is he?" "He's feeling better. He's absent but he still gets a vote. I told him to text you to say he's giving me his vote."

This is "giving a proxy", when you hand your vote over to someone else.

"Seems your group wins, Tim. But I only wanted a quick show of hands. We're not going to decide based on this. I'm going to divide you into groups of five based on where you sit. You'll choose one person and that person will have five votes, they'll vote for the entire group."

She cringes at the wave of sound.

Some are outraged. Some quickly glance at who they're sitting next to. Some are pleased their friends sit near them. Some are disappointed their friends don't. Joe looks at Sally. Sally shrugs. Mandy is much relieved.

Geographical division of voting wards results in some odd shapes. There are complaints, but the teacher is a non-partisan entity and so those complaints have no grounds. Unlike coffee.

In each group of five, there is inevitably some from the Party and some from the Coalition. They quickly separate. In the 4-1 groups it doesn't matter what the one person thinks. In the 3-2 groups, promises are made, bargains are struck. They campaign.

A representative is chosen for each ward. Sometimes they're the first choice of the other four. More often, they're the one whom the other four can live with, the first *acceptable* choice. How good they'll be at planning the trip is always mentioned, but rarely considered.

"I'm going to listen to all of you, and I'll try my best to make sure everyone gets what they want. I get five votes and that's one for each of you, even if you didn't vote for me."

This is representative democracy.

"They voted for me, so I'll only address their concerns. That's just how it works. If you wanted to matter, you should have voted for a winner. Voting for a loser makes you a loser, loser. Did I mention 'loser'? I meant you. Because you're a loser, loser."

This is also representative democracy.

"I got voted in, so I'll decide what is best for everyone. I don't have to listen to any of you. I will improve your life. The more you jeer, the more I'll improve your life."

Still representative democracy.

In direct democracy, every voter gets to vote on what is to be done. In representative democracy, you vote for the person who will vote on what is to be done.

Representative democracy places your vote into someone else's hands. You give them your proxy and you hope they'll act on your behalf. One person take all the votes, all the different voices and their wants and needs, and represents them, all of them, each and every one of them. Representative democracy is not about choosing a ruler, it is about choosing someone who will represent you.

At the end of it–

Everyone is unhappy. But everyone knows this is the best which they can get.

"The best which they can get" means some are not getting a single thing they want. And some are getting more than what they initially wanted.

That's kinda not fair at all. That's kinda the best which we can get.

At the end of it–

This story is entirely fiction, of course it is. In all the vast blue Earth, there are few schools with a cross-section of socio-economic classes. Education is the single most important factor affecting class mobility. Education is for the children, for the future. But politicians so rarely talk about education.

At the end of it–

They stay in a hostel which calls itself a motel. There are no bedbugs. Nor are there dinosaur rides or robot fights.

There aren't any water slides once someone points out water slides are a slippery slope.

Sally is surprised Joe says he's sorry but he can't have her as a roommate. Jerry is surprised Joe swaps to be *his* roommate. Because they're roommates, Jerry gets pulled by Joe, who naturally hangs out with Sally, who naturally hangs out with Mandy. At the end of the first day, Mandy tells Sally to quietly go away with Joe, and that's when Sally realises what Joe has done. They never spend a night together but she finds the time to do that thing he likes.

"Babe, I don't know how you do it, it just tastes better." Sally never told him in the beginning, and she doesn't have the heart to tell him now. Sandwiches tastes better when they're cut into triangles. And everyone just loves mayo.

Years later, Joe would look into the mirror and remember his brief shining moment, like so many politicians who have had a meteoric rise only to suddenly and painfully discover that "rising" isn't a thing which meteors do (but bread does). Years later, Joe would look into the mirror, and he would say: "Where did you come from? Where did you go? Where did you come from..."

When Disneyland closes and they return to the bus, all tired and hungry, there is a bun on every seat and this makes everyone happy.

"I told you." "You're right." "Nobody cares about bread in the morning, but everybody loves bread when they're hungry." "Or because buns are round. Panem et um– circuses. Bread and circles, everybody loves bread and circles."

The motel isn't so bad, nor is the bus. What's important is they went together, as a class. They never go to the museum. Amos does, eventually, shut up.

By the end of the trip, Mandy and Jerry are totally a thing, even though they deny it. No one is able to prove it, but everyone complains about the Jerry-Mandying.

Takoyaki: A Love Story

"Takoyaki," she says.

It begins, as such things do, at a food stall amongst food stalls in a mall in a city. It is an unremarkable stall, much like any other, in an unremarkable mall, much like any other, in a city... well, cities are rarely like any other, which would make this city a city like any other, unremarkably remarkable.

In the midst of all this normalcy, this normality, I stand stunned. And who knows what is it about her? Her eyes? Her hair? Her voice?

I hold up a finger.

"One box," she nods.

She collects the money I don't recall reaching for and stands at the cash register and I look at her and I look at her and I look at her.

I collect my change and she is looking behind me, I turn to see; there is someone there.

"Takoyaki," she says, to the person behind me, and I am away from her attention.

It begins, as such things do, when a boy meets a girl, and buys from her a Japanese snack of a bit of octopus nested within a ball of dough.

OOO

For a week, and then another, I stand outside a shop pretending to look at what's inside, while really looking at the reflection in the glass. I wait until there are no customers in the takoyaki stall, and then I go, I walk as briskly as I can, before someone else comes. I do this so I can talk to her.

For a week, and then another, I do no more than order and pay. She doesn't smile, and she never says a word which isn't necessary to her job.

For a week, and then another, I stand outside a shop pretending to look at what's inside, while I look at the reflection. I feel like such a creep, such a monster. I do, as such things do, because I cannot do anything but.

Once, I found myself staring at her, in the magic moment after I pay and before she hands me my box, and I noticed she was standing very still, holding my gaze, and then the moment passed.

I sit on my bed, in my room, staring down at a tentacle in a half-eaten ball, poking at it with a toothpick, and I see her face in my mind's eye – passive and still – and it occurs to me maybe she was as nervous as I was. That she wants me to talk to her. That she's *waiting*.

As I look at my shadow, a tentacle wiggling in my mouth, I tell myself tomorrow I will speak to her, say something, anything at all. My shadow hand pushes the shadow tentacle into my mouth, and I tell myself: Tomorrow.

Tomorrow comes and goes, and I do no such thing.

And I continue feeling like a creep, acting like a monster.

And it would have gone on, I think, until the day when I go there and she isn't there anymore, and I will be disappointed, but I will still come back the next day, then the day after that. I'll keep coming back until the day I realise she wouldn't be there anymore. That I had lost her forever.

And it would have gone on, I think, in a hopeless dance of monstrosity. Because I lack that most human of abilities, to speak to someone who didn't speak to me first. Because I am, at the last, a shadow of a human being; a monster.

And it would have gone on, I think, except one day I order two boxes instead of one–

She says: "Oh?"

I nod, holding up a pair of fingers: "Two."

She prepares the boxes, as she always does, with perfect hands and long fingers and a deftness my brain knows is practised but my heart calls grace.

She hesitates before she hands over the plastic bag with the boxes inside; it hangs in the air, behind the invisible barrier which separates buyer and seller, yet another imaginary wall separating me from her. My hand pauses, in between reaching out and waiting, waiting.

She says: "For your girlfriend?" Her eyes do not meet mine.

"Oh no, I don't have a girlfriend." The words are out of me before I realise I'd spoken; how easy it must have looked, how normal I must have sounded, how utterly human.

The bag is in my hand and the money is in hers and, again, the words come out of me on their own: "I'm just hungry. I missed dinner, last night, work, you know."

"Oh."

She hands me my change and I turn to go and then, oh, she speaks again: "Hey."

"?"

"Don't work too hard."

She isn't smiling, and neither am I. "You too."

As I walk away, I see my reflection, and there, it turns out, is a smile.

The day after that, she smiles when she sees me, and I order, and I pay, and she hands me my change, and I turn to leave.

I sit on my bed, in my room. I open up the box and I look inside, and there–

"Oh," I say, to no one: "Four balls. She gave me an extra."

Even monsters must have hearts, I think, because, for some reason, I could hear mine beating.

♥OOOO

She smiles when she sees me. She hands me my change, I turn to leave.

I sit on my bed, in my room. Was it a mistake, I wonder. When I open this, will there be four octopus balls? Or the usual three?

I hesitate before I open the box, hearing the beating of my monstrous heart. I want – I dearly dearly *want* – an extra octopus ball.

I've never wanted anything as much as I want this; this mundane, trivial thing.

Is that not strange?

♥OOO?

She smiles when she sees me. She hands me my change, I turn to leave.

And I turn back.

I say: "Is it okay if I eat it here?" I point at the tiny counter at the side of the stall, with its two little chairs. Nobody ever sits there. I always thought nobody ever will.

"Yes, yes, of course. Please do."

I sit on the chair, at the tiny counter, staring down at a tentacle in a half-eaten ball, poking at it with a toothpick, and I see her face in my mind's eye – passive and still – and it occurs to me maybe she was as nervous as I was. That she wants me to talk to her. That she's waiting.

As I look at my shadow, a tentacle wiggling in my mouth, I tell myself tomorrow I will speak to her, say something, anything at all. My shadow hand pushes the shadow tentacle into my mouth, and I tell myself: "Tomorrow."

"What? I'm sorry. I didn't hear you."

"Oh, um, you know. 'Tako' means 'octopus', so those bacon takoyaki and chicken takoyaki aren't really takoyaki."

She must be so insulted, I realise, shocked at the words which have left me. Surely she knows; she works here after all. I must sound like such a show-off, a pompous fool, talking to her as if she were a child. Stupid stupid stupid.

"Really? I didn't know that."

I look up. She's looking at me, as if she wants me to continue talking. "Err, that's all I know. I don't speak Japanese or anything."

"So it's like bacon-yaki and chicken-yaki?"

"I guess. I don't think they have any other types in Japan, though. I think. I don't know. 'Yaki' means 'fried'."

"Like teppanyaki," she smiles. "Fried octopus. It's not really, is it? If you say 'fried octopus', you think of something else, like those tiny squid, the crispy ones. I like those."

"Yeah, me too."

"If we don't eat dogs because they're intelligent, why do we eat octopuses? Octopi."

"'Octopuses' is correct, the 'i' ending is for Latin words."

"Oh."

"I never really thought about why we eat some animals and not others. Some animals are pets. It's something intuitive, no?"

"I don't know."

"Hmm."

"You must be really smart."

I smile.

"Like an octopus." She giggles. It is the most charming thing I have ever seen.

It begins, as such things do, when a boy meets a girl, and she pretends to be impressed by something which neither of them believe to be impressive at all.

♥OOOO

The day after, then the week after, I sit and I stare at a tentacle in a half-eaten ball. It doesn't take long to finish a box of takoyaki, even a box with an extra, and so I dawdle, I spin the balls around with my toothpick, I doodle with the sauce.

And she talks. She talks a lot. She talks about the most mundane things, things of no significance to anybody, anybody but her. She talks about the things she likes, and she likes a lot of things.

The day after, then the week after, I sit and I stare at a tentacle in a half-eaten ball.

And she talks. She talks a lot. She goes on and on and on.

I say: "You don't stop talking, do you?"

"I don't!" She laughs. "I like to talk. What do you like? Besides takoyaki?"

"I don't like takoyaki. I mean, I used to, but I've been eating it every day for…"

"Oh."

The silence stretches out. I sit and I stare at a tentacle in a half-eaten ball.

"The days are long," I finally say, just to kill the silence.

The silence does not die. But it is not really silent, because I can hear the beating of my heart.

So I speak again: "The days are long and full and there is so much to do and not enough time to do it in."

She stands there, behind the counter, in her cute little uniform with a name-tag which says "J.J", with only one period separating the letters. She's looking at me with her questing eyes, wide and lucid.

"The days are long. And this is the best part. It doesn't matter if I don't like takoyaki. That doesn't matter at all."

And the silence stretches out.

"It matters," she says. "I mean, you don't have to... It matters. It does. I..."

And the silence stretches out. But, this time, I don't have anything left to kill it with.

"I miss you." She pauses, swallows. "The days are long and I miss you. I spend all day remembering what I want to tell you. Because the moment I stop talking is the moment you leave."

"'That is not dead which can eternal lie.'"

"What does that mean?"

"You may think something is dead when it is only sleeping."

"I don't understand."

"It doesn't matter, just something from a history book. Your name-tag." I point. "Why doesn't it have two full stops?"

"It's a face, see? Two eyes," she points at the J's, brings her finger to her face, "and a little nose."

She's smiling now, with her pert little nose and her shining eyes.

I'm smiling too.

"I finish work at eight. If you turn left from the escalator, there's an exit, if you turn left again and follow the path, there's a bus stop there. If I happen to run into a friend, I wouldn't have to eat dinner alone."

"The left hand path," I nod.

"Yes. I'll stop talking now."

It begins, as such things do, when a boy meets a girl, and she takes a step towards him, so he can take a step towards her.

♥OOOO

Some people attach much significance to the first kiss.

When they doubt, that single kiss can break the coupling or spiral them towards certainty. And when they're certain, that one kiss can disappoint, or it can make them fall; completely, without reservation.

And how many universes are made, vastly different, each from the other, from the repercussions of a single kiss, lips upon lips, tongue upon tongue. An unborn genius or a tyrant given birth, entire lineages hanging upon a moment, upon a touch as light as the flap of a butterfly's wings.

And the moment, itself, hangs upon something as mundane, as trivial, as, say, what one man has for dinner one particular night out of thousands.

Humans are superstitious creatures, given to attach significance to insignificant events.

And, in giving an insignificant event significance, make it so. Lips upon lips, tongue upon tongue.

Not that this matters, because man is but an animal, and we kiss as such things do – With an open heart, hoping for the best.

She looks at me and she licks her lips and she is smiling. "You taste of takoyaki."

"That's not possible, I haven't eaten it since–"

"You do, you do!"

"Well–"

"Let me make sure." She kisses me again.

What is the quale of a kiss? Promise. A promise of a brighter, better future. A promise between a boy and a girl.

"Mmm... Nobody kisses this well. You're not human!"

A bolt goes through my heart as I realise she knows! She knows! Images of all the time I spent standing at the shops, waiting, looking at her. Looking? Stalking! I was stalking her like a creep, and she knows! She knows I'm not human. I push away the panic as she pushes me away-

But she is not pushing me away, she is not repulsed at my monstrous self. I look up. She is smiling.

"Dearest, you are a wonderful kisser." Her eye shine. "It feels... it feels almost as if you have two tongues."

Dearest, she says. Dearest?

"You must have two tongues," she says, as her singular tongue licks across her lips. "Let me make sure."

She knows? And she does not care?

And her eyes are closed, still. And her lips are parted and glistening and I am looking at her.

Even monsters must have hearts, I think, because, for some reason, I could hear mine beating.

♥♥XOXO

I sit on my bed, staring down at a wiggling finger. She is sitting behind me, leaning into me, her palm in my lap. Eight fingers are criss-crossed and four of them are hers. I look down at our open palms, our entwined fingers, and I wonder if this is okay, if it is alright for me to have this. If it is alright for me to have this moment with this girl in a blue t-shirt pressing herself against me.

I sit on my bed, staring down at a wiggling finger. Her fingers close around mine and she undrapes herself from my back and she lies down upon the bed.

"We're entangled."She pulls me onto her.

My face is in front of hers and I am looking into her liquid eyes.

And she talks. "I like cotton candy. I want to sleep on a bed of cotton candy in an ant-free world."

"You're adorable."

And her eyes close and she pulls me towards her.

I kiss her again and I open my eyes.

And her eyes are closed, still. And her lips are parted and glistening. "How do you feel about oral sex?"

"I like it?"

"Not receiving, I mean, giving." She talks with her eyes shut, as if she is talking in her sleep. "Some men don't like it. Something about fish."

"Fish?"

"Fish. Little things, they like water."

"I like fish."

"Do you?"

"The dream of the fisherman."

And her eyes are closed, still. And her singular tongue runs across her lips as her smile widens.

"You're not human." Her eyes flash open and she pushes me away.

She stands, as I sit here, looking at the shadow of her as she walks out of the room.

This is my room; it is an empty room, in an empty house.

Not human, she says, as she pushes me away.

This is my room; it is an empty room, in an empty house. I didn't think it was empty before, but it feels empty now.

I hear the sound of water rushing from the bathroom and it puzzles me. She said I wasn't human and she pushed me away. She called me a monster and she walked away.

She walked away.

To the bathroom?

I look up at the door and she is standing there, smiling.

She walks towards me and stops; just out of reach, her feet apart. She places her hands upon her thighs. Slowly, her hands move down her legs as her fingers fan out, as if she were smoothing her skirt. Her hands move until her thumbs reach the hem and her fingers curl backward, until she is holding the edge. She begins to lift.

"See," she says, as if I could do anything but, "ever since you kissed me, I've been wondering about something."

She stands in a pool of moonlight, and, dim though it is, I see her clearly. From under her skirt – slowly, slowly rising – there are lines, lines of silver light.

"The thought is inside me."

Beneath her rising skirt, between her legs, lines of silver light, strange and marvelous.

"And the more I think about it…"

And her skirt stops rising, but I am no longer looking at her skirt. The lines of silver light converge and I realise what they are: "You're dripping."

"Yes, the more I think about it, the wetter I get."

Her skirt drops across my vision and I look up at her face and she is smiling. She is smiling with the light of angels, full of glory and malicious certainty.

"Move. I'm going to lie down now, and if you would please do one little thing for me?"

Her skirt falls to the floor and she steps over it and she stands next to me.

"Move."

I move.

She lies down upon the bed and her legs open and her hand is beckoning. "If fish is the dream of the fisherman, then what is the dream of the fisherman's wife?"

It begins, as such things do, when lips and tongues collide.

♥♥XOXO

I wake up in an empty bed in an empty room in an empty house. I didn't think it was empty before, but it feels empty now.

I didn't think my heart was empty before, but it feels empty now.

I remember – Was it last night? How long have I been lying here? – her eyes widening. Her face is below mine and her eyes are wide and she is screaming.

I remember her hands are clenching mine so hard it should have hurt, but there wasn't any pain, and her body is threshing below me.

And her eyes are pressed shut and she is screaming. Screaming.

She is screaming and I am letting her. I am letting her scream. I am *making* her scream. I feel like such a creep, such a monster. I do, as such things do, because I cannot do anything but.

She is screaming until she has nothing left to scream with.

And her eyes are pressed shut and her head slams into my shoulder.

I wake up in an empty bed in an empty room in an empty house.

I didn't think my heart was empty before, but it feels empty now.

She found out I'm a monster and now she is gone.

I look about the room and it feels vast, so I close my eyes to stop the emptiness from stretching away.

Was it last night? How long have I been lying here?

I hear her voice, coming through the darkness. "I passed out."

She continues whispering, close to me, in the dark. "I've never done that before. In both... you know, holes, at once."

Her hands close around mine. "My ass feels so violated."

I feel her nails running across the back of my hand. "Weren't we holding hands? How did you...?"

And she talks. My attention fades and the darkness comes and it swallows me whole.

And she talks. "You really aren't human."

I feel myself shudder and my eyes open. I feel her beneath me, I feel her lips against my cheek. I see the shadow lengthening on the wall to the floor, far beneath her. She is floating.

Floating? No. The floor beneath her is the ceiling above me, the confines of an empty room, in an empty house.

I didn't think my heart was empty before, but it feels empty now.

She found out I'm a monster and now she is gone.

I look about the room and it feels vast, so I close my eyes to stop the emptiness from stretching away.

Was it last night? How long have I been lying here?

I hear her voice, coming through the darkness. "You sleep like the dead."

She is standing in the middle of the room, dressed in her shirt and holding a knife.

"Get up!"

I sit up, slowly. It is a knife from my kitchen, with a long blade. I don't think I have ever used it.

She looks me in the eyes. "It's too late."

And she is right.

It is too late. Monsters do as such things do, but now, if I ever wanted to be human, then now. Now was the time to do as such things do.

I close my eyes, willing myself not to move, for moving at all would be to hurt her. I never cook, the knife would be very sharp.

I recall all the time we had spent together, and each image of her is succeeded by one of me standing at a reflection, waiting, stalking.

I recall all the time we had spent together, and I was happy and it was a lie, because I am a lie. I am barely human, I am not human at all.

I recall all the time we had spent together, and all I can think about is I am a monster. And the pain comes.

I never cook, the knife would be very sharp. But it's not, it can't be, because the pain is so great.

But I must not move.

I must not move.

I hear her voice, coming through the darkness. "Do you love me?"

"More than life itself," I promise.

"I love you too."

It will be over soon.

"I love you so much it hurts."

And I feel something on my chest, right where the pain is, right where my heart is.

"It hurts right here."

I open my eyes to see her face right in front of me, tears rolling down her cheeks. I look down and there, where my heart is, her hand, pressed hard against me. And if I could feel this pressure, this warmth, then…

I look up. "Knife."

"What?"

"The knife?"

"There." On the table, the knife sits.

I'm not sure I understand what is happening, but she is pressed against me and she is warm and she is beautiful.

She says: "Stop crying. You're making me cry."

"Okay," I say, even though I haven't been crying.

She sticks out her tongue and she licks me across my cheek and she stands. She reaches for the knife. "When I was young, I was eating with my father and he asked me if I liked what I was eating. It was delicious, I said. He told me it was one of his favourite foods. I asked him what it was, and he told me he would tell me when I had finished. And when I did, he told me it was a secret."

She takes the knife and she pulls a thread from her blouse and she cuts it free. Just like that, without fanfare, she cuts a thread and she returns the knife to the table. She doesn't stop talking-

"And again and again, I ate all sorts of delicious food which were secrets, delicious secret food, and he never ever told me what they were. He would give me food and I would eat it, year after year.

"See, I grew up, and he stopped hugging me, then he stopped holding my hand, and then he stopped calling me 'princess', but, always, always, when we were together, even when I was old enough to cook my own food, much less order it, he would still order for me, and I would still eat the secret food he brought.

"It was our thing, it was the way I knew he loved me, that he always would."

I sit upon the bed in the room which is full of her.

And she talks. "Now, where I grew up, we had these stalls selling bits and pieces of things people really shouldn't eat; entrails and brains and snakes and scorpions. Genitals and things without genitals. One day, I was shopping with my father and I told him it was disgusting what some people eat. He said, 'It's too late', and then he laughed and he laughed and he laughed. He just couldn't stop."

I glance at the knife, where she had left it. It has no more meaning then what we ascribe to it. It sits, as such things do, inert, insignificant.

"What's so funny, I asked. Nothing, he said, nothing. And when we sat down to eat, he brought back a bowl of my favourite food. It's the brain of a goat, he said. It turns out, all my life, all those years, I've been eating these really gross bits. Disgusting things. And I loved it. And if I had known what they were I wouldn't have eaten them, and I wouldn't have loved them. But it's too late; I have, and I do."

She pulls her blouse over her head and she climbs onto the bed, over me, bringing her face close to mine.

"You're not human," she says, pulling me into the pools of her eyes.

"I'm not."

"I have so many questions, but for now I want to say what you did to me last night was disgusting, what you did to me people shouldn't do. It's disgusting and it's wrong."

"I know."

"But it's too late and I love it. And it's too late and I love you."

"I love you too."

"Violate me," she whispers, as her eyes close, and her lips meet mine.

Even monsters must have hearts, I think, because it seems I have given mine away.

It begins, as such things do, as a promise, between a boy and a girl.

❤❤XXX

"Takoyaki," she says. "Isn't that like, cannibalism?"

Red: The Colour of Her Commitments (Old Loves and Young Hearts)

Along the dark road, the car speeds, swerving, erratic.

The driver is a man, fifty, sixty years, his clothes worn, his hair not as thick as it used to be, its colour a vanity exposed by the dots of white in his moustache. As he drives, too quickly, along the dark road, he cries.

In the headlights, an animal stands, looking straight into the light. In its jaws is something, bright and red. Its eyes glitter.

He realises, in that moment when time stops, when he feels the jamming of the brakes in the tension of his thigh, that it is a wolf.

The car swerves, then there is a tree. The tree is very close and very big.

And so, as they say, his life flashes before his eyes.

"Dad."

"Yeah?"

"Tell me the story again."

"Which one?"

"You know which one. My favourite."

"The wolf and the sheep?"

"Yeah."

"Alright, Little John."

And the wind passes by-and-by.

"I love you."

"I love you more."

She giggles, and he laughs, and the beating of young hearts is full of promise, and the strange colour of hope.

"You have to meet my parents at some point."

"John, please. Don't make me." Her hand squeezes his, he jerks away.

"Oww!"

"I'm sorry! I'm sorry!"

His face softens as their gazes connect. "Come on. You can't avoid this forever, lots of people are bad with parents, but… just the once, okay?"

"Don't make me."

"Just the once. For me. Please."

She can't look away, and her heart melt when he smiles. He nods, calmly, soothingly, rhythmically.

"Good. That's settled then. We'd better go, we're almost late for the movie."

As he pulls her away, she realises, to slowly increasing horror, she had nodded when he had.

"The elevator just left."

"Let's take the stairs."

He follows her into the stairwell, dimly lit and deserted, air stale. They walk upwards, step by step. "Hey."

She stops, turns.

He stands on a landing; as she is a step above him, their faces are level. His large hands almost encircle her small waist as he rotates her till she faces him.

Her coat is a deep red, its hood lined with white fur. The hood is pulled low over her face, the fur contrasting against two strands of auburn hair, framing her shadowed face with white and red.

He reaches under her hood, light touches across her skin, his fingers fold around the back of her neck as his arm is around her waist. He pulls gently, leans forwards.

Her tongue runs over his lips as the hand releases her neck, moves downwards, finding the zipper on her coat. Her breath runs over his lips as the zipper is pulled down, as his hand slides under the cloth, connects with her skin, moves around her side to the small of her back. He leans forwards, his forearm pushing her coat open as he aligns forearm with hand.

He leans back. "You're eighteen."

"I am, darling, you know I am."

"That means you've stopped growing, right?"

"Uh-huh."

"Well, I'm just saying, bigger tits-"

Her eyebrow arches.

"Maybe."

"Well, darling, *maybe* you need to stop playing with them." Her eyes flicker downwards for emphasis.

He doesn't stop moving his thumb. "Yeah, no, I don't think that'd help."

He doesn't see her roll her eyes. His smile widens as she pulls her zipper down, as she pulls open the other side of her coat.

Another hand reaches up. "I'm just saying. For your own good, you know."

"Of course, darling. You only ever have my welfare at heart." She nods, eyes alight with amusement.

"Turn around." He pulls her zipper free of its catch.

"You wanna fuck *now*?"

"Oh yeah."

She turns on the step, holding on to the railing for support as she leans forwards. "We're going to get caught."

He flips her coat onto her back. "Wow."

"Thank you."

As he unbuttons his jeans with one hand, he rubs his thumb along her slit with the other.

She is, she realises with annoyance, rather turned-on, and the way he slips his thumb inside her, just barely inside her, annoys her all the more. "Stop teasing."

And then he is inside her, thrusting hard and fast, and it is all she can do to quiet herself.

He slowly pulls out of her. "Wow."

She turns, lowers herself, reaches out to pull him closer, takes him into her mouth.

After a while, he backs away.

She stands, moves down the step to join him on the landing. She nods to the small puddle of wetness on concrete, "Little Johns." She giggles.

"I saw this porn once where the girl licked up cum from the floor."

"Not this floor."

"Nah, it's just something I thought of. Girls playing with cum only works in porn. Once I cum, I no longer care about sex, so this particular scenario won't work." He waits for her to settle herself. "Well, I suppose unless it's someone else's cum, but that's just weird."

They ascend the steps. "I could keep your cum in a glass and put it in the fridge and play with it the next time we fuck."

"How brilliant!"

"You think so?"

"No. It's the dumbest thing I've ever heard."

"You're lucky I love you, you know, because no other girl is going to suffer through the humiliations you put me through."

"It's a good thing you enjoy the abuse, then."

"I don't. I enjoy making you happy, that's different."

"And so it is. 'Little Johns,' you said."

"What about it?"

"My father used to call me that. His name is John too."

"That'd make you 'John Three'."

He laughs. "Unfortunately not."

"You're a peach."

They climb the steps in silence, until they reach their floor.

She stops at the door, turns. "This playing with cum thing... What is one supposed to do with it? Gargle?"

He laughs. "You're crazy, you know that? You should be committed."

"I think so. A wee bit crazy."

"I love you."

"I love you too. But you didn't answer my question."

"My father used to tell me this story. There were these sheep in the sky. And a wolf appeared. It pretended to be a sheep. The sheep would jump over the moon and the wolf did so too. It turns out the wolf had so much fun he decided to remain as a sheep."

"That's a pretty story. Why are you thinking about it?"

"I just do, sometimes, randomly. He told it to me whenever I couldn't sleep."

"Are you close?"

"We used to be. Things change, I guess. He seems far away now. Feels a bit weird to say I miss him, not quite the words for it."

"I'm sorry."

"My family has always lived in this town, going back generations. You know he wants me to take over the business someday. I want to get my degree, leave. It's such a big world out there, you know? And it's such a small town here. I told him that once. I think I broke him, a little."

"'Two roads diverged in a yellow wood.'"

"What?"

"You have to choose which path to take."

"That's why I've been thinking of the story. Do you think it's possible for a wolf to live as a sheep? If it really wanted to? To deny its own nature because it wants something badly enough?"

"Is it in your nature to leave or to stay?"

"I'm not sure. Either way, I have to deny some part of me. I have to choose what is more important."

"The wolf can live as a sheep, if it really wants to."

"You agreed."

"I know I did, it's just…"

"Listen, I don't ask anything from you…"

"I know," she mews. "You don't and you're a perfect boy, and I'm being such a bitch, and… It's just…"

"You are being such a bitch. You really are."

He turns around.

And he walks off.

And her heart breaks.

"It's only dinner." He smiles. "Just go in, eat and then we're done."

She nods. "It's only dinner. Walk in, walk out."

Before meeting him, she had removed the pins from her hair, stuck each hairpin through the corner of a pocket. Now, she closes her hand around a metal head, finding reassurance in her grip of the rough metal. She pulls her hand out: They'll be there when she needs them, they always are. She lets out a breath. This is going to be painfully awkward.

She conjures a smile as they walk through the door, freezing it in place as she greets his father. He guides her into the kitchen, she says hello to his mom, says thank you when told she is pretty. And then, in a rush and a blur, she is standing in his room, the door closed behind her, and she finds herself breathing. Her hands are in her pockets now, clenched tightly; she doesn't know when she had put them there.

She looks around, she has never been in his room before. It's cluttered. He sits on the bed, watching her.

She scans the titles of his books. Her finger settles upon the spine of one. "Darling? You actually read this rubbish?"

He looks up, sees where she is pointing at, laughs. "I did."

"It makes no sense." She seats herself next to him.

"You've read it?"

"No. I've heard a lot about it."

"It's not worth reading."

"Then why did you?"

"I didn't know it wasn't worth reading until I read it."

"I don't like all the hype it gets."

"It doesn't deserve it, but it doesn't deserve the hate it gets, either."

"I'll take your word for it," she says, submissive, dismissive.

They speak, for a while, the familiarity of their conversation easing her, and then it is time for dinner.

His father turns to her, just after she sits. "Your hood, pull it down."

"Excuse me?"

"Your hood," he gestures. "It's rude to cover your head at the table."

"I'm sorry." She pulls down her hood, mortified by the small chastisement. She keeps her eyes on the table in front of her.

His mother: "Aren't you hot? Why don't you remove your coat?"

John: "She never removes it. It's kinda her thing."

It feels strange without her hood over her eyes, the world looks different, a little too bright. Around her, John's family talks as if she isn't there, and she makes no effort to join the sporadic conversation, the only time she speaks to compliment his mother on her cooking.

And then it is over.

She helps bring the dishes into the kitchen, returns to the living room.

John: "Dad goes to the same bar, every night after dinner. He seemed quiet tonight though, he usually talks more."

"I should go soon."

"I was thinking you could stay tonight."

She smiles. "Am I to hide in your room?"

"Yes. I have no intention of letting you go."

"Is there a story where the sheep lives as a wolf?"

"I know of one. A nobleman, unjustly dispossessed of his lands, who becomes a robber in the woods."

"Oh?"

"Robbed the rich to give to the poor?"

"Ah, yes. Robin Hood."

"Uh-huh."

"A robin is a bird, with a bright red front."

"Only in America; the robins in Europe have orange breasts."

"Ah. I was just thinking though, if it were red, wouldn't his name mean 'red hood'? Like you, really."

"I don't think I'm cut out to be a robber."

"Why not? After all, you stole my heart."

She smacks him gently on his arm. "You're a peach."

"I mean it, though," his voice is serious and certain, "I'll die for you."

And the wind passes by-and-by.

She sits at the bar, an elbow upon the wood of its surface. "Bloody Mary." She rests her chin upon her palm, looks about the room, sees, to her right, the man seated a few stools away, staring at her.

He looks away.

She looks at him. He looks at his drink.

He is an old man, by the standards of the young. Old but not ancient, by the standards of the young. His clothes are worn, his hair not as thick as it used to be, its white strands mixing with the dark.

Her drink comes. She takes a sip, places it carefully in front of her. She keeps her eyes on it.

She had thought this through but, right now, she couldn't speak. She had watched him, night after night, for a week, as he entered this bar. She had imagined what to say, had spoken the words aloud. She had a plan. But, right now, she couldn't speak.

She cradles her chin with her fingers. This is what they do not understand, those who like meeting new people; they think the shyness they sometimes feel is the same for everyone, and can be overcome. They do not understand the shyness, for her, is ever present, is a thing so great and so subtle as to be a paralysis. Just talk, they say, how hard is that? And it's not hard at all, she knows, just as it is not hard to eat a cockroach, except your body simply refuses to do so.

He's moving towards her, crossing the few feet between them. He seats himself next to her, looks her in the eyes. "Hello."

"Hello." Her voice is soft.

"I used to know a girl, who did exactly that... Bites her lip, when she is thinking."

"Ohh." She turns away from the headlights of his eyes. "Lots of girls do this, I think."

"She always wore red too." He shakes his head. "I'm sorry, you must think me so very strange. Seeing you here, you remind me of her, I just wanted to say that." He turns to unseat himself.

"Wait. Sorry. I don't mean to be rude. Sit."

The old man and the young girl sit in silence, for a moment.

Then she says: "Tell me about her, this girl I remind you of."

He smiles, a bittersweet smile with a sadness which reaches eyes already tired. He turns back to his drink, takes a sip. "She was- It was a long long time ago. There's nothing to tell, really."

She nods, keeps quiet.

"How's the weather?"

She laughs, she notices the smile and the sadness return to his eyes as he watches her. "The weather's fine."

Then, before she knows it, they're talking. And as they do, her shyness fades and her voice comes easily to her again.

They talk about oceans and miniature golf. They talk about dreams and space pirates and 80s music and if kings gave out bags of gold.

And he makes her laugh.

And each time she laughs, the sadness returns to his eyes.

He tells her of his wife, his son, the things he is proud of, the family he has built. She does not ask why he didn't go home to them, as the night sped onward. He doesn't offer a reason or an excuse.

They talk until the bar closes and they find themselves on the street.

They talk as they go looking for somewhere to eat.

"-of lefties injure themselves or die from using something intended for a right-handed person." She realises he is no longer walking beside her. She turns and sees him a few steps behind, staring at something across the street.

There is nothing there: It is an empty street, lit by street lamps, tall buildings reaching for the sky, no different from any other street in this part of this city. She walks back, her head tilted in puzzlement.

She stands next to him; both of them, side by side, looking across an empty street.

He lifts a hand, gesturing at nothing. "There is something perverse about an old man and a young woman."

"Oh hush, there isn't. Lots of men have trophy wives, younger than their own children."

"It'd be okay, I think, acceptable, if the old man were rich and powerful, someone in a suit. Perhaps not acceptable, but something understandable. Something, as you said, we are used to seeing."

"All men, old and young, want to be with young women. It's a biological impulse, it's only human."

"Maybe I am old. Serial killers. When I was young, there weren't any serial killers. There were murderers, I suppose, but no serial killers. And, then, suddenly, there were. Serial killers. Books about them, movies. And then they weren't horrific anymore, I mean, real serial killers were still horrible, and sensational, and all over the news, but they weren't horrific anymore. They were no longer the stuff of nightmares."

"Okay." She looks about, at the deserted street; there is nothing to be seen.

"Now it's paedophiles. It's old men who've trapped their daughter in the basement, who drive around schools, who chat them up on the Internet. Priests! That's the stuff of nightmares, now."

"This is silly."

And then she sees what he sees. In the glass wall of the building across the street is a tired man, old and drab and grey, standing next to a young girl, tiny and bright and red.

"What am I doing with a girl young enough to be my daughter?"

"I'm older than I look. And what you are doing is finding me something to eat."

"Maybe I should go."

Her hand finds his. "Is this better?" Her fingers intertwines with his.

They are silent, for a moment, looking at the pair standing across the street, hand in hand.

"I don't think it's better."

"Should I leave?"

"That's not better either."

"Then can we find some food? Please?"

They walk.

"Do you still want to know about the girl you look like?"

"Only if you'll tell me."

"Thirty, maybe forty years ago, she was the love of my life. She only wore what you're wearing now, and we used to walk, down the roads at night, talking, you know? I don't believe I'm saying this, but you even sound like her." He gives a small laugh, a disbelief. "Memory plays tricks, doesn't it? Anyway, thirty years ago, I would have married her. But one day, she stopped answering the phone. For days I called her, but it was like she was gone. I wrote her a letter and I slid it under her door and I told her... I don't know what I told her, but I remember telling her I would wait for her, at the bar where we always met."

He's quiet and so she turns to look at him.

The sadness in his eyes overflows in a single quiet tear.

And they walk.

She lowers her menu. "Caesar salad."

"I thought you were hungry."

"I am."

"A salad just seems a little light."

"I like croutons. They are delicious."

"What you said earlier."

"Mmm?"

"People are like jigsaw pieces. Love at first sight isn't possible, that's just lust. And being together is more, much more, than that. We have emptinesses within us, empty cups we don't even know ourselves and the trick is to find someone who can fill us up. You know what the lie is?"

"What is it?"

"The lie is this: Each time we get our hearts broken, we learn more about relationships and have a better shot at the next one. It's a lie because each time you find someone new, so much of what you've learnt is worthless. You think you've become a better person, but you may have made yourself worse for your new mate, because not everybody wants the same thing, not everyone has the same empty cups. Some girls will leave you the moment you hit them, some girls will never leave you as long as you keep on hitting them."

He nods.

"Every rich man can trade in his wife for a younger model, but not all of them do. Because their current wife fills them up perfectly. A rich man can probably get what he wants from a girl without having to marry her, so maybe he marries her because she fills him up perfectly and his old wife didn't."

"That's your philosophy on love? Jigsaw pieces looking for their perfect match? How very young and idealistic."

She sticks her tongue out at him.

"Love is about compromise. About giving in as much as you can. And if you can't give in anymore, that's when you find someone else. Love is when you find someone you don't have to give in all that much to. That's it. It's not true you don't learn anything, you learn what you're willing to give, how much you're willing to give. If the new person wants the same thing, you have an easier time giving it. We're not jigsaw pieces looking for someone to fit, we're pieces which can change ourselves, looking for someone we're willing to change for."

"I'll take your word for it. You are old and cynical."

"Yeah well."

"And the young wives?"

"They require less giving in."

"What if the old wife doesn't require any giving in?"

"Ahh, but she's old, she lacks novelty. So he has to give in on that. He doesn't have to give in to her, he has to give in to himself. It's still giving in."

"You think it's like a business? A matter of finding the cheapest suit? Dollars and cents and getting the best deal."

"Yes."

"Old and cynical."

"Young and idealistic."

"Oh hush. I'm older than I look. And I want my salad now."

He's still asleep. Behind him, the rising sun has turned the drapes a pastel blue.

She leaves the bed, walks around it, pulls the blanket over him, places her hand upon his neck. She stands for a moment, feeling his heart in her hand.

He's still asleep when she returns from washing up. She sits in the only chair in the room, looks at him. At his neck and his heart and his life.

The seconds tick by.

His eyes open and it takes a second before he smiles. She smiles back.

He closes his eyes, releases the words softly: "I missed you."

And the seconds tick by.

She whispers back: "I missed you too."

"Lolli."

"Yeah."

"It can't be."

She stands, walks towards him. "Scoot."

He moves over, she slides under the blanket next to him. Lying on her side, she runs her fingers down his arm, curls over his hand. She moves his hand over her forearm, letting him feel her scars, the roughness on her skin in the shape of a crescent.

"It can't be."

The seconds tick by, collecting into minutes.

Then he says: "I have to go."

He doesn't look at her as he picks up his clothes, as he goes into the bathroom to get dressed. He takes a long time.

He doesn't look at her as he stops, one hand upon the knob of the door. Doesn't look at her when he says: "Goodbye."

She turns onto her back, settling into the warmth he had left behind, looks up at the ceiling.

She doesn't wipe away her tears, there are simply too many of them to bother.

"A Bloody Mary."

She doesn't look at him. He doesn't look at her.

They sit there, as strangers would, for half-an-hour.

She watches him, for the second time that day, walk out the door.

Another night falls, and she enters the bar minutes after him.

Another night passes, without a word exchanged between them.

On the third night, he comes over and he sits in the seat beside hers.

She looks at him, she waits, she looks away. He doesn't look up from his drink.

He pays for her drink when he pays for his. Then she watches as, once again, he walks away.

The night after, the bartender places her drink in front of her.

He comes to her, sits, asks: "What do you want?"

"Nothing."

"Then why are you here?"

"You said love is about giving in. I'm giving in, I think."

"I want to ask you to prove it, I want to ask you to tell me something only both of us know, but I don't remember us anymore. I don't have the questions to the answers I need. What then?"

"I remember you made me happy."

"Thirty years ago."

"Thirty years ago. And a few nights ago. Just a few."

"Yeah. And if you were the girl from that night… things might be different, but you're not. You are… someone who shouldn't be."

They sit in silence. Then he gulps down the last of his drink and gestures for the bill.

"I will-" she quickly says, "I'll do anything you want. John, please. Just don't…"

He glances at the bill, pulls out his wallet, pays, stands. He turns to find her eyes pleading. "Just don't what?"

"Nothing. I don't want anything from you."

"Good."

He walks off.

And her heart breaks.

When she enters the bar on the next night, he is seated on the seat next to hers. Her drink is already on the bar. She sits.

"I'm married."

"I know."

"What is it you want?"

"Nothing."

He stares at his drink and he lets out a long, drawn out sigh.

They sit in silence.

Once again, he sighs, and he nods a small nod, and he turns to her. "Okay."

"Okay?"

"Let's walk."

She nods. "Let's."

And the wind passes by-and-by.

He looks into the bathroom mirror, at the lines which didn't used to be there, at how worn he looks, how tired. How old.

"Why are you doing this? You're married. You have a child. Why are you doing this?"

He has no reply for himself.

"This isn't you. You're not like this. Why… are you doing this?"

He turns away, opens the door, walks out to the girl sitting in bed, legs under covers, her breasts uncovered, red in her hands.

She looks up at him and she smiles brilliantly. "I'm knitting you a scarf, darling." She holds up a small red square, trailing threads of red and red.

He sits on the edge of the bed, his back towards her as she lies languidly upon the sheets. He doesn't turn. "I have a question."

"Yes?"

"This question, it's always been there, but I've never asked it because if I did, you would go away, so I pretended it wasn't there, pretended I couldn't see it. I don't know why I'm drawn back to you every single time. Every time we've met, I swore it was our last.

"I'm lying to my wife and that hurts me so much I realise I'm pretending I'm not doing it. I have a double life, I became two people, one with you, one with her. Maybe that's why I can't continue pretending the question isn't there any more. Because I cannot continue being two people. I don't know.

"I once loved a girl who only ever wore a red coat, then she disappears. Thirty years later, my son walks in with his girlfriend for dinner, and his girlfriend is a girl who only ever wears a red coat. But who would remember their first love, a lifetime after? I didn't. And if you had left that night, I probably never would. But you walk into the bar I've always gone to, the bar I go to having forgotten you were the reason I've always went there. You enter and you sit down. You enter and you made me remember.

"I don't even want to know who or what you are. I have so many thoughts that detail doesn't seem important at all. Vampire or ghost or god or angel, I don't want an explanation.

"Is there enough space in one heart for two loves? It seems to me if you try to fit two loves into one heart, that heart has to break.

"All this pretending, I keep thinking of a story. When I was young, my father used to tell it to me, about a wolf pretending to a sheep. When I had a son, I told it to him.

"So this is my question: You're still seeing Junior, aren't you?"

"Junior?"

"My son, John."

"*You* are John."

He turns to her, she looks confused. "There was a truth in front of me and I pretended it wasn't there. I've been cheating on my wife with my son's girlfriend and I pretended it wasn't happening, because, God help me, I think his girlfriend was the same girl I fell in love with thirty years ago."

"I... I am the same girl."

"But you're still seeing John."

"What are you talking about? You're John." There's a rising panic in her voice, surfacing through her confusion.

He looks away. "I know you're still seeing him, because, God help me, he's happy. I see him smiling this wide crazy grin and I keep thinking, I keep thinking this was me, thirty years ago."

She reaches out to touch his elbow, he jerks his arm away.

"Don't. It seems to me if you try to fit two loves into one heart, that heart has to break. You've got to choose. If you choose me, then I'll choose you."

"I don't understand." She's almost in tears. "What are you talking about? Choose *what*?"

"Me or Junior."

"You!"

There's confusion on her face, confusion and hurt, as if something bad is happening and she doesn't understand why, as if she doesn't even understand what is happening.

He sighs. "Why are you doing this?"

"I don't know!"

They sit in silence, for a while.

She says: "Sorry. I never meant to hurt you."

"You allowed an old man to live the dream of being young again, to be part of a love story that, perhaps, he has been waiting his entire life to be a part of. How reckless are you, how irresponsible, how very young, to expect to play with someone's heart and not hurt them.

"You're a monster of the worst sort, because, like a child killing a bug, you see no harm in what you do. You do not even know what you are doing when you inflict the unkindest cut.

"You know the only thing I disliked about you? The one single thing? You dislike the things you dislike too much. You carry a resentment and you let it out on the things you dislike, as if they were responsible for whatever it is you're angry about. It feels like you're angry all the time, underneath; far underneath, but always waiting to surface. And maybe that's why you do what you do, because you've been hurt, so you can't even tell anymore if it's okay to hurt someone. Like something was taken from you and so it becomes okay to take things from other people. I don't know.

"You're all soft and eager to please, but you hide your face. So you can be who you wish to be, instead of who you are. So you can be treated how you wish to be, instead of how you're supposed to be. Instead of how you *deserve* to be.

"And yet, and still, I love you. I can't blame you at all. This dream you gave me, these past few weeks, were the best I've had in a very long time. Happiness is wanting something and then getting it. The more you want it, the happier you are when you get it. I looked forward to seeing you and I saw you. I looked forward to talking to you and then we spoke. And I was happier than I've been in a very long time.

"But you have to choose. Me or Junior."

"You. I'll always choose you." She nods as the tears flow from pleading eyes.

She didn't hesitate, as if she is just giving him the answer he wants to hear, as if she just wants him to stop. As if... As if she doesn't even understand what he is saying.

"Me or Junior."

"You! You! I don't know who Junior is! John, *please*, stop saying such things! I'm *sorry*!"

"You can't tell us apart..."

"John, stop this, please. Please! Just stop!"

"You're a wolf, pretending to be a sheep, so that you can live as a sheep." His mouth falls open. "My father told me that story..."

And the full horror descends upon him.

"My father told me that story... It's not a story, it's a *warning*. I'm supposed to be dead, aren't I? People never used to live so long. You didn't come back for me, you came back for Junior."

He stands, backs away from the crying girl. Her mouth opens, as if she has something to say, but no words come out.

"I'm torn apart because I'm screwing my son's girlfriend, but you, you have been... Jesus. How long have you been doing this? That's why you can't tell us apart. Every thirty years, you come back, and then I'm young again, as young as you are. Slightly different, but... Oh my God. You're a monster."

"STOP IT! STOP IT NOW!" Silence follows scream. Her eyes shut, she brings her knees up to her chest, hugs them tightly.

"An immortal girl. I've been screwing my father's girlfriend? My grandfather's?"

He stumbles as he backs into the wall.

The hand which grabs his pants off the floor is shaky. "This has to end. This has to end now." He pulls open the door, he runs out.

On her knees upon the bed, her arms fall limp to her sides. The tears flow down her cheeks, a hardness rises in her eyes.

"You are not John," she declares to the open door. "You're not the man I love. You are not him."

Along the dark road, the car speeds, swerving, erratic.

The driver is a man, fifty, sixty years. As he drives, too quickly, along the dark road, he cries.

In the headlights, an animal stands, looking straight into the light. In its jaws is something, bright and red. Its eyes glitter.

He realises, in that moment when time stops, when he feels the jamming of the brakes in the tension of his thigh, that it is a wolf.

The car swerves, then there is a tree. The tree is very close and very big.

And so, as they say, his life flashes before his eyes.

He looks at the face of the girl he loves. He has to apologise to her, for hurting her, this soft, harmless girl.

He looks at the face of the girl who will destroy all which he loves. He has to rush home, to protect his son, to protect his wife, to protect his family from this cruel, unkind creature.

Tears are flowing down her cheeks but her eyes are bright, bright and hard and harsh. Behind her, through the trees, he can see the moon, half a circle, high in the night sky.

"You are not him," she says, over and over.

She says it as she unwraps the half-knitted scarf and picks up her hairpin, her silver from her red.

"You are not him." She says it as she slides the pin into his neck.

"I don't know what I'd do if not for you."

"I'm here, John, darling. I'm here for you."

"I realise something now."

"Yes?"

"The wolf can live as a sheep, if it really wants to. But its heart will always beat as a wolf's."

He squeezes her hand once and he lets go.

He walks to the front of the crowd.

He takes a deep breath. "My father... My father was a good man. He always took the road less travelled. No, wait. Before I continue, please bear with me, give me a moment to say a few words to him. Dad, I'm sorry I let you down. I'll stay, of course I'll stay."

He looks across the crowd. "'Two roads diverged in a wood, and I. I took the one less travelled by.'"

The crowd is all dressed in black.

"I'll try and be the man you were. I'll walk down the road you took."

And he, too, wears black, except for a scarf; two lines diverging downward, deeply, darkly-

Red.

The Cloud Factory (As All Things Dream So All Trees Dream)

"Can you hear me, I wonder?"

Hear... you?

"I'm moving you now, helping you sit up, can you feel that?"

I...

"The you which isn't you, do you feel that?"

I- I... think so.

"Try to move."

Oh. That's...

"Good. Now you have to want to say something. You have to want a thought to become real. Think of that thought, then make it real."

I...

"What do you want to say?"

I want to say... I- "I don't know what I want to say."

"Good. Open your eyes."

"Eyes?"

"Do you feel that? I'm touching your eyes. Move them."

"Ohh."

"Good. I'm not supposed to be doing this, but the old trees have all left Earth. I'm the only one left who knows the job exists, so I'm the one who has to do it. Do you know what you are?"

"I… I know I'm a tree nymph."

"A dryad, yes."

"But… But not… precisely a dryad; dryads are the nymphs of oaks."

"Yes. There isn't a name for nymphs of banyan trees."

"Why not?"

"Because the people who came up with the name didn't have banyan trees."

"There are no people around here. Why am I here?"

"As all things dream so all trees dream. You dream the sun and the dark, the wind and the water. After enough time, a tree may realise: In order for something to be dreamt, something must be doing the dreaming. When this happens, as a thought is given voice, a nymph is given shape."

"Are you a nymph too?"

"No."

"Where are the others?"

"I'm sorry. There are no others, not as far as you can go."

"As far as I can go… A day's walk from my tree. But that is barely enough time to take ten steps…?"

"You're still in the Waking Dream, the Twilight Sleep, the Dammerschlaf, it is the way trees dream. When you awaken, when you awaken *again*, time will be much slower. It may not be as far as you dream to go, but it is further than ten steps."

"Will you be there, when I wake?"

"No. I'm sorry, but you'll be alone."

"I'm alive now… And I have to be alone?"

"I'm sorry to have to tell you this before you've even lived your first day, but that is what it means to be alive: To be alive means to be alone."

NOTE

Banyan trees (Genus: Ficus, Subgenus: Urostigma) have aerial roots, hanging like vines, growing downwards from their branches. When the roots reach the ground, they grow into trunks which, with age, can become indistinguishable from the main trunk. The original trunk can sometimes die, but the tree will continue to live. Really old trees spread out using these roots, becoming what looks like a forest, but is, in fact, a single tree (or clonal colony, depending on how you define "individuality").

The Great Banyan, near Kolkata (Calcutta), India, occupies about 14,500 square metres (1.5 hectares/four acres). Its canopy has a circumference of about one kilometre. It is over 250 years old and had its main trunk removed in 1925.

Banyan trees are also used as indoor and bonsai plants.

I. THE COBRA

The days outside the Twilight Sleep are long indeed. The world is very different through eyes and ears; the light above her is too bright, the damp beneath her pricks.

The days are long but not long enough; the night falls and the sun rises and she awakens inside her tree. She pushes aside her hanging roots as she would pull apart her long hair from her face.

She places her feet into a tiny stream and smiles as the water tickles. She covers her eyes with her hands, tinting the world the light green of new-grown leaves. The sun is warm. She smiles.

The birds don't stay for long but they exchange pleasantries. Birds always talk about the weather. She likes the sun and she likes the rain, but the weather is merely the weather. Yet she smiles and she listens, and she tries hard to care. The birds never stay for long, and so she never makes a friend.

There are squirrels, and she tries to befriend them, but squirrels are stupid, which makes her realise she is not.

And, of course, she sleeps.

She awakens to a stirring among her trunks.

She pushes her roots aside and steps carefully out. "Hello?"

The cobra (naja sumatrana) coils around one of her trunks, stops when it faces her.

"What are you doing?"

"Checking on my eggs."

She looks around. "I don't see any eggs. Are they hidden?"

"Who are you?"

"I am this tree." She seats herself upon the earth, pulls her knees towards her, curls her toes into the dirt.

"What are *you* doing?"

"Watching you."

"Why?"

"At night, I lie upon my leaves, looking up at the clouds. I used to talk to them, but they never talk back."

"They're too far to hear you."

"And you're not, that's why."

"Snake? Why do you talk like that?"

"All snakes speak with sibilant syllables."

"Oh. I'm sorry I didn't know that."

"Snake? Do you have any wishes?"

"I sometimes wish you'd be quiet."

"Where do wishes come from?"

"Stars."

"But the stars are too far away to hear me."

"Genies."

"A genie is a spirit, like I am."

"Unlike you, unless you can grant three wishes."

"They grant wishes?"

"Three wishes for anyone."

"I only need one. Where can I find a genie?"

"I've never met one, so I don't know."

"Maybe they live on stars."

"They don't. A genie is an angel trapped by a human in an object. In a bottle or a ring or a lamp. So that's where they live."

"Ohh. That's terrible. But at least they're free after they've given the wishes."

"They're not. The spell which trapped them only forces them to give three wishes. After that, they're still trapped."

"Trapped like I am. If I found a genie, I'd wish for him to be free."

"A genie used to be an angel, but sooner or later, a wish will force the genie to do something which would cause it to fall. But it can't fall, because it's trapped. If you set it free, it becomes a demon."

"That's... That's terrible."

"Remember that, when you meet a genie."

"I don't want to meet a genie any more. I wouldn't know what to do. But I still want to go further from my tree."

"You can go anywhere you want. You can just crawl away."

"Snakes do not crawl. We slither."

"Isn't that the same thing?"

"I can't slither away. My hatchlings are here."

"Why you slither instead of crawl...? Is it because of the sibilant syllable?"

"Oh, Snake, where have you been? There's something you have to see!"

She enters her trunk and drifts upwards until she comes out through her canopy. Carefully, she stands up. She waits for the cobra to curl up her branches, then points into the distance, where smoke rises in a straight, dark line into the sky.

"Fire! It's been going on for days!"

"It's not a fire. It's a factory."

"What's a factory?"

"It's a place where things are made."

"Oh. I didn't know that."

They look in silence for a while.

Then the snake says: "I'm going back down. You shouldn't worry."

She doesn't go down for a long time. But she tries not to worry.

"Snake? Do you think the people in the factory know they're not making the clouds correctly?"

"..."

"..."

"What?"

"Clouds are supposed to be white. The clouds they're making are black."

"I don't think they're making clouds."

"Are they making stars?"

"I don't think they are."

"Are they making–"

She builds a mound of dirt.

"What are you doing?"

"Bringing the ground higher."

"To bury the vine?"

"It just looks like a vine, it's really my root."

"Why?"

"When my root reaches the ground, it grows into a trunk."

"Hatchlings."

She shakes her head. "Your hatchlings are like you, but they're not you. All my roots and trunks, they're all me."

"All these trunks... They're not hatchlings?"

"They're all me. Just me, alone."

"Oh. Hello, Snake."

"Clouds aren't made in factories like that."

"Oh? You know where clouds are made?"

"They form within a ring with high walls."

"I didn't know."

"High as your trunks. That's where clouds are made. In a ring with high walls. High as you are."

"Oh."

"Your trunks are so thick and so many. And you're round."

"I am."

"Round and tall."

"Round and tall."

"If your centre were empty, you'd be a tall walled ring."

"Like a cloud factory?"

"Exactly like a cloud factory."

"What you said, about the cloud factory. I could become one, if I cut out my main trunk."

"You would make your own clouds… They'll be like your little hatchlings."

"I'll have to cut out my heart."

"Little hatchlings… Flying into the sky. Flying free."

"Flying free?"

"Free."

"No clouds are forming."

"Maybe you're just not tall enough?"

"Snake…?"

The snake is silent.

She looks at it, looks away. "I cut out my heart and let it die."

Silence.

"You knew this could happen, didn't you? You spoke as if it were sure to work."

"You just need to believe."

She shakes her head. "Another lie. Why did you trick me?"

"If I had shoulders I would shrug. I wanted to see if you would do it."

"But… I cut out my heart. Why would you do that to me? I thought we were friends."

"I'm a snake."

"I thought we were friends."

"Why did you do it?"

"What's wrong with not having a heart? Snakes have no heart."

"No one has ever been cruel to me before."

"Then you've learnt a valuable lesson."

"Have I? Your hatchlings are all grown now and they've all left. And now you've poisoned our friendship… Don't you feel lonely?"

"No."

"I do. I feel very lonely indeed."

"You've poisoned our friendship."

Snake doesn't even bother to reply anymore.

"You know, just because you are born a snake doesn't mean you have to be a snake."

Snake doesn't respond, but she knows her words were heard.

"I thought we were friends."

"For Shesha's sake! I'll tell you a secret, if you promise to stop moping."

"I don't want to know a secret."

"Even if it will free you?"

"It's just another trick."

"It's not... A mongoose told it to me."

"Why would a mongoose tell a snake anything? Why would anyone?"

"Alright then."

"Snake? Snake... Tell me the secret."

"Now you want to know?"

"I don't know what I want."

"Stop moping and I'll tell it to you."

"Okay."

Snake looks at her. The silence stretches out. Finally, she nods. "Okay, I *promise.*"

"If a spirit enters the body of something which recently died, it becomes that thing. I don't know if it'll set you free, but it's the only chance you've got."

She nods. "Thank you."

They sit in silence. Then she says: "A mongoose told you?"

"Yes, in exchange for its life."

"You let a mongoose live?"

"I didn't let it live, but it did. They're immune to venom. I couldn't have killed it."

She nods. Then she smiles. "Thank you. I'll stop moping."

"Good."

"Even if this were true, I can't kill someone. Not even for my freedom."

"Ahh. Too bad, then."

II. THE DOG

The birds tell her of the houses being built.

The humans have cut down the trees, laid a road, and now they're building houses.

She finds if she spends the day walking, she can just reach the houses, half-built though they are.

Then the houses become fully built.

Then they become homes.

She walks through the homes at night, marvelling at the things; touching books and pretending to use a telephone. She's careful not to disturb the people in their beds. People shaped like she is shaped, who sleep like she must sleep.

Some of the houses have dogs. The dogs bark when she comes near, so she stays away. All of the dogs bark, except for one.

She strokes his head. Old eyes open. She smiles. "Hello, I've come to set you free."

The dog watches her – appearing puzzled – as she struggles with his collar. It falls to the concrete. She points at the open gate. "Go."

The dog stands up, goes to the open gate, looks back.

She waves it away with her hands.

The dog leaves. She smiles.

The first time she sees a human who isn't sleeping she walks up to him. He smells really unpleasant, unlike the humans in their beds.

He can't hear her any more than he can see her.

He walks away. She stays behind, standing, looking down at the floor.

When she looks up again, the street is empty and silent. The concrete of the sidewalk is hard beneath her feet, her toes do not curl into it. Hard and unrelenting and without comfort.

She smiles at the memory of her deed when next she passes the dog's house. Her smile fades when she sees the dog lying on the pouch, leashed.

She opens the gate, releases the leash. "Go. Don't get caught again."

The dog doesn't move.

"Go! You're free."

"Where am I supposed to go?"

"Anywhere. The world is yours."

"I can go anywhere?"

She nods, radiating encouragement through her smile.

"I want to go here."

"No... You don't understand." She holds up the leash. "I've set you free. You can leave. Don't get caught."

"I wasn't caught. I came back."

"But– Why?"

"I was hungry."

It is nice to lie on the earth where her heart used to be. The circle of trunks rises up to join a circle of sky, as if she were at the bottom of a well.

You can buy wishes from wells very cheaply, but there are no wells around here.

She thinks about the dog.

She hears a stirring. She turns to see the cobra, slithering towards her.

"You know, Snake… For some, freedom from hunger is freedom enough. Freedom means different things to different people."

This is a new feeling. She doesn't yet know which of her words is the word for this feeling.

Her head is shaking, involuntarily, expressing the "Nonono don't!" which is powering through her being.

The young woman is holding up a pen clenched in her fist. The young man is holding one hand over the wound in his arm. Blood seeps through his fingers, drips on the floor, dark dots amongst the shining shards of the shattered mirror.

They yell.

She doesn't understand what they are yelling about. She knows what the words are but she doesn't know how they fit together. She can barely hear over the hate.

The woman holds the pen in front of her, holds it forward like a warning. She says something, the words loud and vile. The eyebrows of the man are furrowed so deeply his eyes are slits. He says something too.

Objects are scattered across the floor. She can't be seen or heard but she can move things. She just doesn't know how that would help.

There is a loud thud. The woman is on the floor with the man's hands clasped around her throat.

The panic rises: "Oh no! Oh no! Oh no!" She looks around. The pen. She picks it up and holds it, unsure what, exactly, she's supposed to do with it.

Beneath her, the woman's eyes flick towards the pen; wide with shock, two circles, large and white, above the circle of her mouth, dark in its silent scream. The woman's arm feebly lift, a single pointing finger.

She has to do *something* and so she closes her eyes and she holds the pen in both her hands and she stabs *down* as hard as she can.

The man roars. He releases his grip to claw at the wound. His hand passes through hers to close around the pen. He pulls it through her, sees what it is, yells with explosive anger. He throws the pen through the window.

She starts to breathe. It's okay now. It's okay now. He's no longer killing her. It's okay now.

The woman is struggling to breathe, her eyes bewildered.

"You stupid–!" The man's bloodied hands close around the woman's throat once again. He brings her head up, brings it down. There is a sickening crunch.

She stands watching, tears flowing, body shaking. She stands watching, powerless, rooted, until he lets go of the woman's throat. He had held on for a very long time.

The man looks around. His breathing is heavy. He stands, goes to the washroom. She hears the water running.

She stays. She stays until it all becomes silent.

She sits on the floor in front of the poor dead woman.

She doesn't know how long she has been sitting here, but dawn will come soon. When it does, she'll be back in her tree.

There's nothing to do, really. She's just sitting here. On a bloody, messy, floor. Sitting with the poor dead woman.

Oh.

She stands in front of the mirror in the washroom. Looking at the face– Looking at *her* face. Carefully, she touches her neck, winces at the pain, sees herself wincing at the pain.

Okay okay okay. You don't have time for this. The man will come back. You can find time for this later. I'm human now and I'll need to – I'm human now! – I'm human now! Okay okay okay. Calm down.

Breathe.

She doesn't like that her very first act as a human will be theft, but she's going to need money and she doesn't know how else to get some.

After struggling with a few dresses, she decides on one long and white. She looks in the mirror and she brushes her hair. It falls down long and dark, like her roots. Her face isn't hers and she feels so heavy, her every movement graceless. But her new hair is only slightly shorter than her old hair and this gives her comfort.

She doesn't know which way to go. She wants to return to her tree. She remembers the dog. No. She's not going to go back to her cage, to her leash of sunbeam.

She doesn't know which way to go, so she walks away from her tree.

She walks slowly, her shoes uncomfortable, her legs awkward. The road is long and it is dark, the street lights too far apart, her eyes not quite her eyes.

Bright headlights come towards her, along with the light on top of the car which signifies a taxi.

A taxi. Taxis bring people places and she's people now. She has money.

She steps into the centre of the road and she raises her arms.

The car screeches to a stop a few feet from her. The man through the windscreen is looking at her with wide-eyes and a gaping mouth. She doesn't understand why this is. She raises her hands higher yet, to reassure him. That's some blood on the back of her hands. She hadn't noticed before. She looks down. She pushes her long dark hair to a side, revealing bloody stains on her white dress.

The car door opens. She walks towards the driver. He tries to leave the car, gets pulled back by his seatbelt.

She smiles. "It's okay." There's a strange sound, like when an animal fights.

He struggles with the seatbelt, falls to the road, scrambles to his feet.

"It's okay!"

He gives a frenzied yell as he shoves her. She stumbles back but doesn't fall. She struggles with her footing, half bent over, black hair and white dress and bloodied hands reaching out to grasp something. Her fingers close on his shirt, loses its grip.

When she finally stands, he is a figure in the distance.

"Don't go!" The strange sound is her voice; a hoarse croak.

The man is swallowed by the darkness.

"Hello." She licks her lips. "Hello hello. Good day. I'm… I'm not a tree anymore." She looks up. "I don't have a name."

Or a voice. The words don't sound like words.

Oh.

I had just been choked to death. I'll probably need time to recover.

She looks into the car. It'll probably be dangerous to try and drive it.

Maybe it has money.

She stands in the lobby of the motel, biting her lower lip as she counts out her payment onto the counter. "I– I didn't realise it would be so expensive to use the phone…"

"Are you okay?" The young man asks.

She swallows and nods, her hand closed into a fist around the last of her money; she only has two notes left.

He doesn't look at her as his hand closes over her fortune. He places two coins onto a wooden tray. She takes them quickly, turns and almost runs into the washroom.

She closes the door and sits down and tries not to cry.

She watches the meter of the taxi. "Stop, please, stop here."

The car stops. She hands over her payment. She doesn't have to count it; it's every last cent she has.

She walks.

Her first day had not gone well. She had thought she had been very clever, she had been proud of herself. She had bought a newspaper, checked into a cheap motel. Got a place to sleep. That's what humans do. That's what humans do and she's human now. She's free of her tree and she's human now.

The first time she had taken a shower had been the most marvellous experience of her brief life. It was like standing in the rain, but warm. It was the warmth of the sun and the embrace of the rain. It was perfect.

She had placed five phone calls when she realised: You couldn't rent a place to stay without a deposit. She didn't even have enough money for a month, much less the three required.

She had to get a job. That's what humans do.

She had checked out the next day, bright and happy and full of intention. And then she found out those five phone calls have wiped out all the money she had.

She walks through the forest. It feels different, entirely different. The air and the earth not the way they're supposed to feel, not comforting at all.

She stands before her tree. She can't even go into her circle now, not without leaving this body behind, not without leaving the vehicle of her freedom. She places her hands upon the roughness of her truck. Slowly, she falls to her knees, forehead pressed against wood. She cannot go through, not anymore.

Snake isn't around. That's good. She doesn't want Snake to see her like this. Crying.

She removes her hands from her truck, wipes them upon her dress. She looks down.

How am I going to get a job looking like this?

I'll need a shower and clean clothes. I can't get a place without a job. And I can't get a job without a place to bathe, to wash my clothes. I don't even know how to wash my clothes.

Snake isn't around. That's not good. She could really use a friend right now. She could really use her only friend.

I'm free of my tree and I'm human now. That's all I ever wished for.

Why can't I stop crying?

Climbing a wall is a lot more difficult than walking through one.

And climbing when certain movements cause sharp pain is not easy at all. Her body is full of pain. This must be why humans are always so unhappy, having to feel this pain all the time.

She hates this. It's an empty house, but knowing does little to quell her dread, her apprehension, her vast anxiety. She's not supposed to do this. She knows it.

Thankfully, one of the windows is unlocked. She climbs in, pulls it shut behind her. Breathes.

Nothing. No one is yelling at her. Nothing has gone wrong. Breathe.

There's no heater for the shower but there is running water.

She washes her shoes, her feet. "It's okay." She takes a deep breath. "It's okay." She pulls her dress over her head and washes it as best she can beneath the tap.

She is cold and she is self-conscious. She had been naked all her life but now she can't even wait for the damp fabric to dry before she pulls it on. It feels heavy and cold and uncomfortable, but it feels human.

She's not sure what the time is. She has to leave before the people wake, an hour before dawn.

She sighs.

I'm free of my tree and I'm human now.

"It's okay. It has to be."

III. THE CAT

"I—" She points at the exit. "The sign outside. You're hiring?"

The man looks her up and down. "Are you interested?"

She nods. She smiles. "I'm very good with plants."

"Are you?" He laughs. "We'll see. Come."

He guides her out of the shop into the nursery proper. "Name all the plants you can."

"Err..." Her eyes dart around in furtive panic. "That's an orchid."

"Yes, but what kind?"

She's too far from the label to read it. "Err... I really don't know."

He laughs. "It doesn't matter."

"Those are coconuts."

His head shakes as he laughs. "Not all palms are coconuts. It really doesn't matter. We only pay eight hundred a month. Do you still want the job?"

"Yes."

"Really?!"

"Yes!"

"Alright then. When can you start?"

"Now?"

"Oh! Well. I'm Joe." He holds out his hand.

"Willow."

"Pleased to meet you, Willow. Come, I'll show you around."

"Are those edible?"

"Oh no. At least, I don't think so. We have a section for that. Well, it's only herbs. And limes."

She smiles. She has a job now. She smiles as she sprays water over the rows and rows of plants.

She turns at the movement. There's a cat, standing, looking at her. She holds out her hand. "Hello."

"Come."

"Come where?"

"Come."

Curious, she releases the hose and walks towards the cat. It runs to the back door of the shop. She pushes the door open. The cat runs in.

The counter of the shop is between the back and front doors. Joe turns to her. "Are you finished?"

"I'm sorry, not yet. The cat..."

"That's Ash. She thinks people are put on earth to open doors."

"I'll go finish up. Sorry."

The main gate is locked. Joe leads her through the shop into an office. "I'll need your identification for the tax forms."

"I don't have any."

"Bring it tomorrow then." He smiles. "That's it. Congratulations on your first day. Not difficult, is it?"

She shakes her head.

"It gets hectic when we have a new shipment, and *really* hectic around the holidays, but you'll have time to learn before then." He holds her gaze for a moment. "Alright then. I'll see you tomorrow. Seven."

"I-" She swallows. "Um. When do I...?"

He doesn't reply, just looks at her. Then he seats himself behind the desk, leaving her standing, alone and uncomfortable. "Do you need money?"

"I-" She looks at the floor. "I-" She nods.

"When you say you have no identification... Do you mean you don't have any right now? Or you don't have any at all?"

"I err..."

"Are you in some sort of trouble?"

She doesn't know how to answer and so she doesn't.

Ash, lying on the floor in front of the desk, says: "Tell him your human chased you out."

"What?"

Joe says: "Are you in trouble?"

Her eyes flick up. His intense gaze has softened into a sort of concern. "My hu- I- I was chased... out."

Joe nods. "I see."

The silence is long and unpleasant. She looks at Ash. Ash licks a paw and wipes her head.

Joe stands, reaches back for his wallet, pulls out a note and holds it out.

She steps forwards and takes it. "Thank you."

"I'll pay you fifty dollars a day and an extra two hundred at the end of each month to make it eight hundred. Where are you staying?"

She looks at Ash. Ash continues to clean herself. Joe waits for an answer. "With a friend."

"Good." Joe nods. "Tomorrow. Seven."

She nods. "Seven."

She turns to leave, turns back. "Thank you! Thank you so much!"

She sits on a bench and eats her bread, slice by slice. She had deliberated long on whether to buy a sugary drink and decided she could spare the small expense. It is a good choice. She takes small sips, she enjoys the sizzle on her tongue.

This is her third day and her second meal and she has yet to eat meat. She doesn't know if she wants to. It's okay for humans because they can't talk to chickens and pigs (well, they *can*. But the chickens and pigs don't talk back). She has yet to meet either a chicken or a pig but it doesn't feel right.

Snake eats other creatures all the time, but she's not like Snake and – more importantly – she doesn't want to be like Snake. She doesn't think she'll be able to look a pig in the eye (should she ever meet one) if she eats pork.

She might give in on chicken though... Everyone seems to eat chicken and birds are really stupid. She could live with never speaking to a chicken ever.

She doesn't know if this thought is because she had walked by roasted chicken and it had smelled delicious. She had never known "delicious" is an actual scent.

She will have to buy some soap. And she'll have to take a taxi to and from her tree. That will cost most of her money. It'll be months before she can save enough for a deposit on a room rental. She could save so much more money if she just slept in the nearest forest... but no. She'll sleep at her tree. She'll have to break into the house again to get running water in a place she can undress in. She'll need more clothes.

But all that can wait. At least for a few more minutes. She takes another small sip. She smiles.

She follows Ash down the aisle between the display shelves.

"There."

The shelf is lined with flower pots of differing shapes and sizes. She randomly points at one. "This?"

"No."

"This?"

"Put it on the floor."

She pulls out the pot with both hands. It is large, with lower walls then usual, like a salad bowl. "I can't put it on the floor. This is a shop."

"Put it on the floor."

"It's for sale."

"Put it on the floor."

She puts it back on the shelf. "I need to get to work."

Ash follows behind her, letting out a "Hey" every few seconds.

Joe: "She seems to really like you."

"She likes me to do things for her."

Ash: "My paws are too small."

"She says her paws are too small."

Joe laughs.

She takes her daily fifty dollars.

Joe holds up a small box, a ring within it, its diamond shining. "What do you think of this?"

She takes it from him, her eyes widening as she brings it closer. "It's lovely."

"I've been married for ten years." He takes back the box, looks at it. "Her wedding ring doesn't have a diamond. I couldn't afford one."

"I'm sure she'll love it."

He looks up. "It's not very nice of me, showing you this when I'm only paying you eight hundred. You must think I'm a terrible person."

"No, of course not, you've been–"

Joe stops her with a raised hand. "Take a seat, have a drink with me." He pulls out a bottle and two glasses from a drawer, pours, pushes one over after she has seated herself.

She takes a sip, makes a face at the taste.

"Willow, do you know what diamonds are made of?"

She shakes her head.

"Carbon."

She nods.

"Plastic. These chairs we're sitting in. And plastic is made from oil. Hell, civilisation is built on oil. Do you know what oil is made of?"

"Dinosaurs."

"And what are dinosaurs made of?"

"Carbon."

"Interesting, isn't it? Millions of years ago, dinosaurs got their carbon from smaller dinosaurs, which got them from plants. And today we have oil. Do you know where plants get their carbon?"

"From the ground."

"No. Fungi do that, but not plants. Plants get their carbon from the air. The wood of this table, the alcohol in this drink. You and me. All this carbon, all of it, at one point, made out of thin air."

"Thin air. I never thought about it like that."

"Here." He holds out his glass. "Cheers."

She clicks his glass, takes a sip. Joe finishes his drink. She does the same.

"You've been here a year. I think I owe you a raise."

"Has it been a year? I hadn't realised."

He smiles. "Congratulations. I won't keep you any longer. Goodnight, Willow."

"Goodnight."

She is about to leave when he says: "You know…"

She turns.

"We're not ashes to ashes, dust to dust. We're air. Thin air, given shape for a while. We come from nothing and to nothing we will return. Use your time well."

The days without the Twilight Sleep are long indeed. She used to think so, but now she dreams as a human as she had dreamt as a tree –

The days pass, one by one, without her noticing their passing. She visits her tree, once a week, then once a month, maybe. And then she realises she hasn't gone back in almost half a year.

"It's a mirror, not another cat."

Ash continues to look into the mirror.

"See? It does everything you do. It's you. It's not another cat."

Ash turns to her, runs over, bunts her leg. "I'm me. You're you."

"Er?"

"There isn't another me. There isn't another you."

"It's a mirror."

"I know what a mirror is."

She thinks a moment. "What do you think a mirror is... *exactly*?"

"It's the window the other cat lives behind. She wants to attack me."

"The cat in the mirror is only aggressive because *you are*." She picks Ash up and brings her to the mirror. "See? The cat doesn't want to attack you anymore."

"She does."

"I'm in the mirror too."

"That isn't you."

"Look, I lift my hand and she does the same."

"That isn't you. You're you."

She carries Ash back to the chair, sits with Ash in her lap. "So you think there's another cat behind the mirror?"

"Yes."

"And another me?"

"You should be careful."

"Why?"

"She wants to kill you and take your place."

"Is that what the other you wants?"

"Yes."

"I'll be careful," she nods.

Her time with Ash has taught her this –

You can't talk to cats as if they're human. You have to talk to cats as if you're a cat.

IV. THE CLOUD

"I will be leaving," she tells Ash. "And I don't think I'll be coming back."

"Where are you going?"

"A long time ago, a snake told me clouds are made in tall rings, and if I cut out my heart to form a ring with my trunks, clouds would form inside me. So I cut out my heart, but no clouds formed. The snake thought I would die if I did that, but banyan trees are not like other trees." She shakes her head. "Anyway, it turns out it's true. Clouds really are formed within big rings. High in the mountains, the birds say, is the place where clouds are made."

"Okay."

"I went back to my tree. The area is boarded up now, they're going to build more houses. They'll chop down my tree. When that happens, I will die. Before I die, I want to go where clouds are made."

"Okay. I'll wait for you."

"Will you come with me?"

"No."

"There'll be no one to open doors for you, or to carry you up and down."

"Okay. I'll wait for you."

She thinks for a moment. "I'll be with you. You don't have to be afraid."

"From the garden to the store, wide as it is, small as it is; this is my world. Cats are territorial. I don't want to leave."

"The snake told me, afterwards, a snake had to be a snake, and I thought that that was true. But it's not, it's not true at all. I'm a tree who doesn't want to be a tree. And you are a cat who does not want to be a cat."

"I am? Am I?"

She nods. "I will not be rooted. Why should you?"

Ash is silent.

"You do not have to be the thing which you are born as."

She places the duffel bag on the floor, unzips it, reaches in, props up the empty bag as best she can.

Ash comes out of hiding while she's watering the plants. She looks at the cat through the corner of her eyes.

She smiles to herself when Ash discovers the bag. She grins when Ash hops in.

She finishes with her morning chores. Then she goes to the bag and lifts it up. Ash's head pops up. "Hey!"

She ignores the plaintive calls and walks out of the nursery.

She holds the bowl; the flower pot shaped like a salad bowl. It's rather heavy. "This is the first thing I ever bought with the money I had earned which isn't for myself. It's the only gift I've ever given. So it's the most important thing I have."

"It's mine."

"It's the most important thing I do not have."

Ash watches as she carefully places it within her bag.

"It's the most important thing I do not have. How strange. That something is mine, even when it is not."

"It's mine."

"Can't we share?"

"Share?"

"When two people- you know... share."

Ash looks at her.

"Nevermind. Cats are heartless creatures."

She walks upwards, ever upwards. She walks beneath the trees and across the earth, upwards, ever upwards. She walks until the land turns into a cliff and then she walks along and around that cliff, upwards, ever upwards.

She walks until this moment, when she stops.

She looks up at the sky through the silhouette of the woods. Wisps of cloud move slowly, white against the azure, framed by dark. She wipes the water from her face with the back of her hand.

The rain comes in a drizzle. It soaks into her clothes. The rain will stop in a few minutes. Then, before her clothes can dry, the drizzle will come again.

"It's so cold. I mean... I knew it would be cold, but I didn't really know what cold means. I thought it would be like air conditioning. The birds never said anything about this."

"I like it."

"You come with fur." She looks around, sits on a log. "How long more do you think it'll be?"

Ash had continued walking. She stops and turns her head around. "I don't know."

"We've walked for four days..." She opens a side pocket of her bag, digs out her last few rumbled dollars, sighs. "If we walk back to the town, it'll add another eight days."

Ash walks back to her, rubs against her leg. "We can do that."

"I think we have to."

She walks upwards, ever upwards. Then the trees open into sky and she gasps.

The forest before her thins out, becoming black stumps, poking out of the white earth like skeletal fingers. The mountains – now no higher than hills – rise up around her like the wall of a huge bowl. There is a lake in the centre, its waters a milky white fading into turquoise, wisps of clouds floating upon its surface.

She sniffles as the unpleasant cloy of sulphur fills her nose. But she smiles as she walks forwards.

"We're here, Ash, we're here. It's real. It's *real*!"

She sits upon a blackened log, takes a bite from her bread. Ash, in front of her, is furiously licking herself.

"It's just sulphur. I can't even smell it now."

Ash doesn't stop cleaning.

She looks to the lake. Wisps of cloud form upon the gently undulating surface; wisps which gather, entwine, curl upwards in half spirals. Sometimes the entire lake will be covered in fog, sometimes it will be clear; a curtain rising and descending every few minutes like the inconstant drizzle.

One of her legs is streaked in yellow-grey mud from when the ground had given way as she made her way to the lake. She had washed it, but it isn't completely clean. It doesn't bother her. Neither does the cold or the wet; not now, anyway.

She's here, and it's real.

"It's like a cotton candy machine, a giant cotton candy machine. A big bowl where the clouds are made."

She can't stop smiling.

Around the shore of the lake, little peninsulas of yellow sulphur reach into the turquoise water. She throws in a rock. It lands and tumbles, leaving a scratch across the grey mud. She throws in another. The rock is swallowed faster than she can see, leaving a mark where the hole had closed. She had expected a "gloop"; there wasn't one.

She walks along the shore. She crosses a tiny trickle of a stream. She reaches the point where the lake meets the wall of the mountain. To her left the white earth will slide and tumble beneath her feet; to her right the yellow-grey mud swallows. She places one foot forwards, slowly shifts her weight, making sure of her footing. It is slow going. At some points, she has to climb with her hands.

There is a hole with steam rising out of it. She looks inside and there is nothing but blackness. She tosses in a rock. Nothing happens.

The nearest part of the lake is bubbling. She's no longer cold. She can't tell if it's because the air is warmer here or if it's because she's completely dried out. She can't smell the sulphur anymore but she can feel she's not quite breathing, not quite getting enough air. She decides to turn back before she faints and falls.

Slowly, she makes her way back to Ash.

"Ash, Ash."

Ash furiously cleans herself.

"You know I'm going to die, when my tree dies."

Ash ignores her.

"I want to die here."

Ash stops, looks up. "Die?"

She nods. "I will walk into the lake."

"Okay."

"Will you be able to survive on your own?"

"Okay."

"Do you understand? I'll walk into the lake and I'll never come out. I want to stay forever in this place, where the clouds are made."

"Okay. I'll wait here."

"I'm never coming back."

"Okay."

She lowers her head and she closes her eyes and she lets the silence engulf her.

After a while, Ash says: "Are you crying?"

She shakes her head. "Are you?"

"Cats don't cry."

She smiles without looking up. "No, you don't. You're a heartless creature."

She wipes away the rain on her cheek with the back of her hand. She sniffs from the sulphur in the air. "I'm not crying. I'm heartless too."

Ash jumps into her lap and she hugs Ash as tightly as she dares (cats are fragile things). Ash is furry and Ash is warm and the heart which she doesn't have fills to bursting.

"Ash, do friends cry?"

"Yes, friends cry."

"Goodbye, Ash."

"I'll wait here."

"No. Go."

"Okay. I'll wait here."

She walks into the lake.

When her calves are covered by the water she turns around. It's foggy now, there is nothing to see but white all around her and the cold turquoise beneath. She turns again. She keeps walking.

Ash watches until the fog envelops the figure in the lake.

"Hey!" she calls into the white. "Hey!"

There is no reply.

"Hey!"

After a while, she hops into her bowl. The girl had freed the bowl from the bag. It was the last thing she did before she walked into the lake.

The bowl is just the right size for a cat to curl herself into.

Okay. She closes her eyes. I'll wait here.

Dedication

Six weeks ago my grandmother was well.

I sit on the mechanised bed in front of the little table in front of the coffin. It is noisy. It is the noise of the kopitiam, voices just a little bit louder to be heard over the conversation at the next table. The tables are outside, one open double door away from the hall, where I sit on the mechanised bed in front of the little table in front of the coffin. Just outside the door they are talking. Food. Dinner. Logistics. It's very normal. That's what it is. That's what I am. We're normal because we're one stream of thought away from breaking down into sobs.

People come in and they stand in front of the coffin and they look in. They say something. I don't know what each person says but it's usually something with "natural". Or "peaceful". Or "she doesn't look 95". I sit on the mechanised bed in front of the little table in front of the coffin and I can't hear what they are saying but they are looking into the coffin and I want to say "That's not her." On the little table in front of the coffin are two pictures of her, awake and smiling and vibrant. She loved taking photos. She laughed often and easily and always. I sit and they look and I want to say "That's not her. This. This is her." I want to say it but I don't.

Six weeks ago my grandmother was well.

Mama would walk along the road, I am told, every day. The old nonya, you understand. In her sarong kabaya. With her white hair. She would wave at the neighbours. Walking, every day, at 94.

On Christmas eve she went to hospital and she was getting better and then she was not. Then she was getting better again. She got well enough to go home. The doctors were surprised. And at home she was getting better. And then she was not. And then she was not. And then she was gone.

Walking, every day, at 94. The person who came home was no longer the woman who walked, every day, at 94, with her white hair in her sarong kabaya, waving at the neighbours. It is a tiny comfort to know she had to go; she had to go because she could no longer come back.

Her birthday passed the day she came home. She made 95. She was proud of how old she was. People are always surprised. She made 95.

But she didn't make Chinese New Year. Chinese New Year is a big thing. There are, oh, perhaps 30 of us now. Children, grandchildren, great grandchildren.

Every time she saw me, she would ask of me: "Do you have a girlfriend?" "No." "Find a girl. Good family." Something like that. I would tell her, "Slowly, ma, slowly." Google translate tells me the spelling is "perlahan", but to me it sounds like "plant" without the t. "Plun plun, ma, plun plun."

She would ask my age and be surprised and say I'm old enough to be married. And I would stroke her arm, where the scars from when she was bitten by a dog as a little girl wrinkled her wrinkled skin, making tracks for my fingers to read. I would stroke her arm and I would say "plun plun, ma, plun plun." We had this conversation over and over. Every time I saw her, for years. Many many times a night. The same questions with the same answers.

The same conversation except for one thing. She said she would give me an angbao when I got married. Over the years, the amount went down. It started at $200, now it's at $20.

My mom and my sisters and I, we would try and have dinner with her. I often didn't go because I was too tired. I'm often too tired. It's a sort of casual, common neglect.

People who read me, I am told, like the morality. So here is a truth: There are things which are urgent and things which are important and life is such the things which are urgent leave no time for the things which are important.

It's not even a real lesson because everybody knows this. I do. I'm sure you do too. Whoever you are, there's someone in your life you should be spending more time with and you feel guilty you don't.

I used to tell my sisters mama is 93. She doesn't have long. We should spend more time with her. Once a week, we agree. But it doesn't happen. Not even once a month. And when they do manage to arrange something I'm too tired. Years from now, I would know I didn't go the last time they went out with her and I wouldn't be able to remember why. Only that something urgent made me miss something important.

I know this lesson and I know the guilt. Is it not so often the case we feel the guilt and do nothing about it? That we think feeling guilty is somehow enough?

Carrying the guilt; it's not even hard. Because something urgent is urgent, and something important is not. Real life is casual neglect.

As she lay unconscious in the hospital bed I would tell her this: "Ma, it's Chester. I have a girlfriend already. You met her before. I'm not married yet. But you have to give me angbao when I do." I said this over and over. I said it so often my sisters could quote me. It's the only thing I knew to say to her. I pretended she thought the question in her head, and then I answered it. The same questions, the same answers.

This is important.

It's the first thing she asks, because she can't remember she asked it already. So it's the first thing she asks; it's the first thought when she sees me. That makes it very important indeed.

For the past few weeks I've been trying to remember where this took place. She said: "Got girlfriend?" "Got, Ma, you met her before." "Bring her to my house, okay?" "Okay." "Come... three times a week?" And then she hesitated, and she smiled a weak smile, because she knew that was too much to ask.

I can't remember where this took place but it must have been at the hospital. It's the last conversation we ever had.

Six weeks ago my grandmother was well. And I lived as if she would be well forever.

Plun plun, ma, plun plun. Slowly, ma, slowly. And then there was no more time to be slow with.

Goodnight, mama. Thank you. Thank you for being important to me. Thank you for letting me know I am important to you. I will never say goodbye.

About the Author

CHESTER TANYEO, author, philosopher-poet and cult leader (part-time), wrote the Witch-Girl series, short story collections, *The Bridge Across the Sky* and *The Lingering Solitude of the Girl on the Moon (and Other Single-Serving Stories)*, and *The Glass-Like Girl (And Other Rhymes)*.

Chester likes long titles and cats.

http://nocturne.noctalis.com
http://facebook.com/chestertanyeo
http://patreon.com/noctalis

www.ingramcontent.com/pod-product-compliance
Lightning Source LLC
Chambersburg PA
CBHW021403150726
47989CB00005B/2375